Jimmy Gownley's

Amelia Rules!™

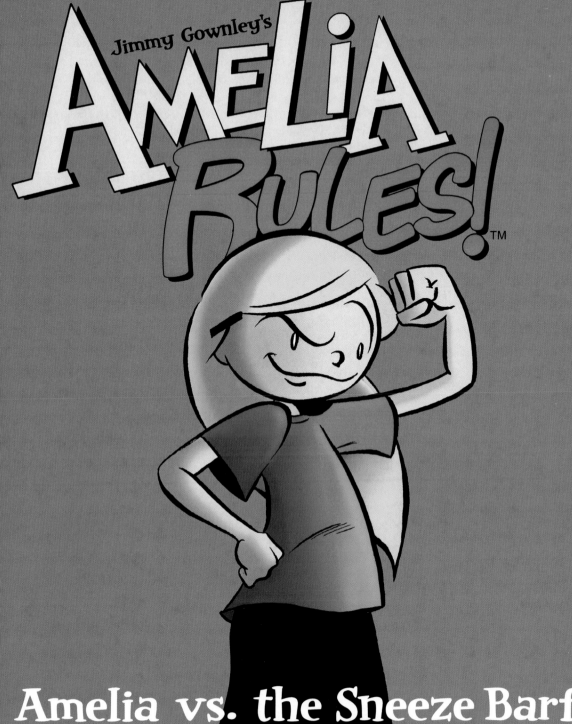

Amelia vs. the Sneeze Barf

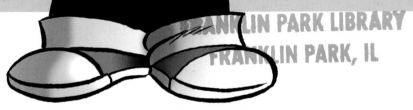

Atheneum Books for Young Readers
New York London Toronto Sydney
Spotlight

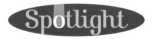

VISIT US AT
www.abdopublishing.com

Reinforced library bound edition published in 2011 by Spotlight, a division of the ABDO Group, 8000 West 78th Street, Edina, Minnesota 55439. Spotlight produces high-quality reinforced library bound editions for schools and libraries. Published by agreement with Atheneum Books for Young Readers, an imprint of Simon & Schuster Children's Publishing Division.

Antheneum Books for Young Readers
An imprint of Simon & Schuster Children's Publishing Division
1230 Avenue of the Americans, New York, NY 10020

Printed in the United States of America, Melrose Park, Illinois.
052010
092010
This book contains at least 10% recycled materials.

Library of Congress Cataloging-in-Publication Data

Gownley, Jimmy.
  Amelia vs. the sneeze barf / Jimmy Gownley. -- Reinforced library bound ed.
    p. cm. -- (Jimmy Gownley's Amelia rules! ; #1)
  Summary: After her parents divorce, Amelia and her mother move a new town where Amelia and her new friends pretend to be superheroes in an attempt to stop the neighborhood bullies.
  ISBN 978-1-59961-787-9
  1. Graphic novels. [1. Graphic novels. 2. Superheroes--Fiction. 3. Bullies--Fiction. 4. Divorce--Fiction.] I. Title. II. Title: Amelia versus the sneeze barf.
  PZ7.7.G69Ap 2010
  741.5'973--dc22

                                                                    2010006192

All Spotlight books have reinforced library bindings and
are manufactured in the United States of America.

With Love and Thanks
to Mom and Dad...

With appreciation for
the Vision and Faith of
Joe, John, Jerry, and Bill...

And with gratitude for
the Patience and Friendship
of Michael...

This book is dedicated with love...
for Karen.

J·GN
AMELIA RULES
399-7155

Amelia vs.
the Sneeze Barf

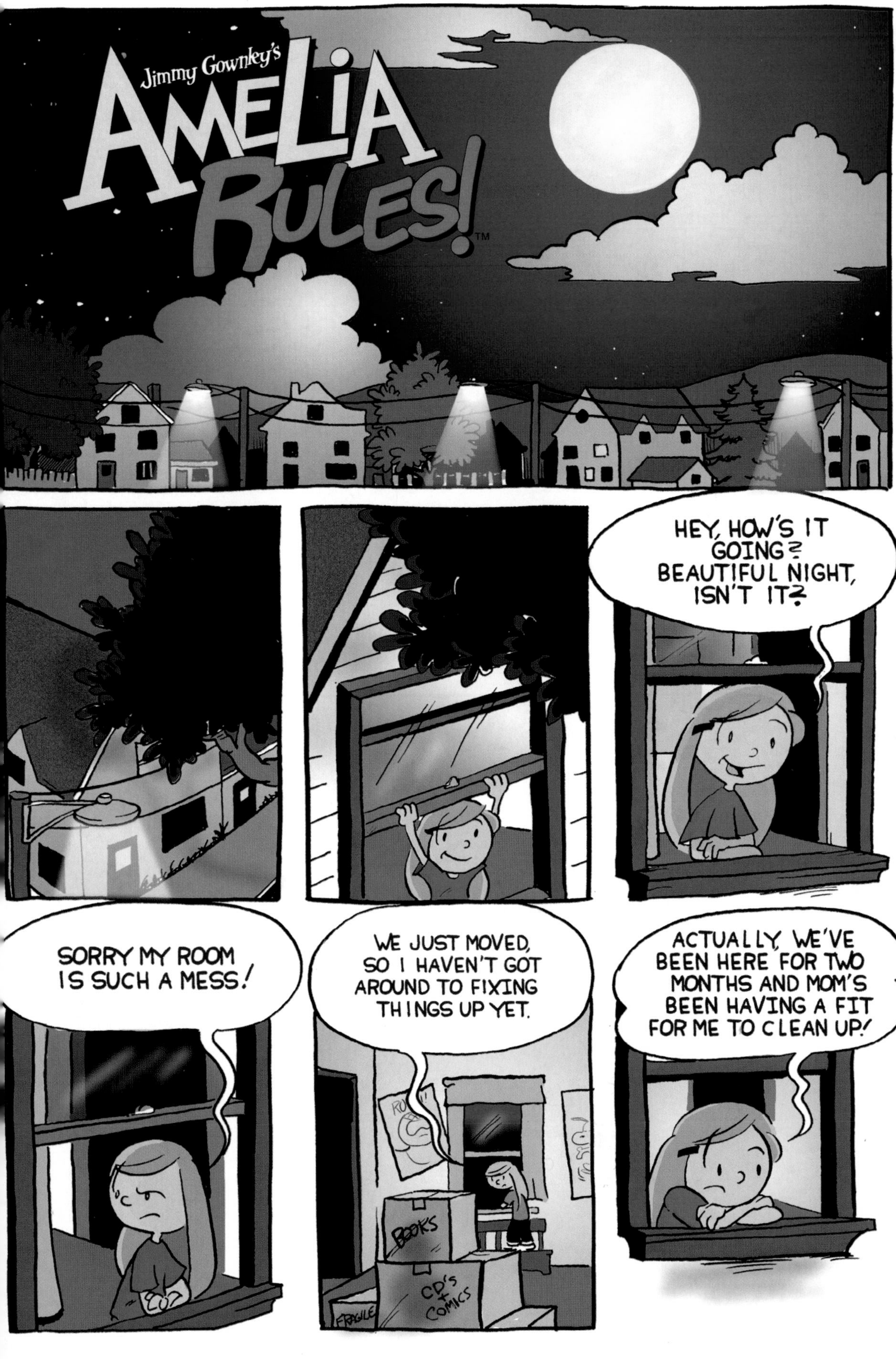
Jimmy Gownley's
AMELIA RULES!™
HEY, HOW'S IT GOING? BEAUTIFUL NIGHT, ISN'T IT?
SORRY MY ROOM IS SUCH A MESS!
WE JUST MOVED, SO I HAVEN'T GOT AROUND TO FIXING THINGS UP YET.
BOOKS
CD'S + COMICS
FRAGILE
ACTUALLY, WE'VE BEEN HERE FOR TWO MONTHS AND MOM'S BEEN HAVING A FIT FOR ME TO CLEAN UP!

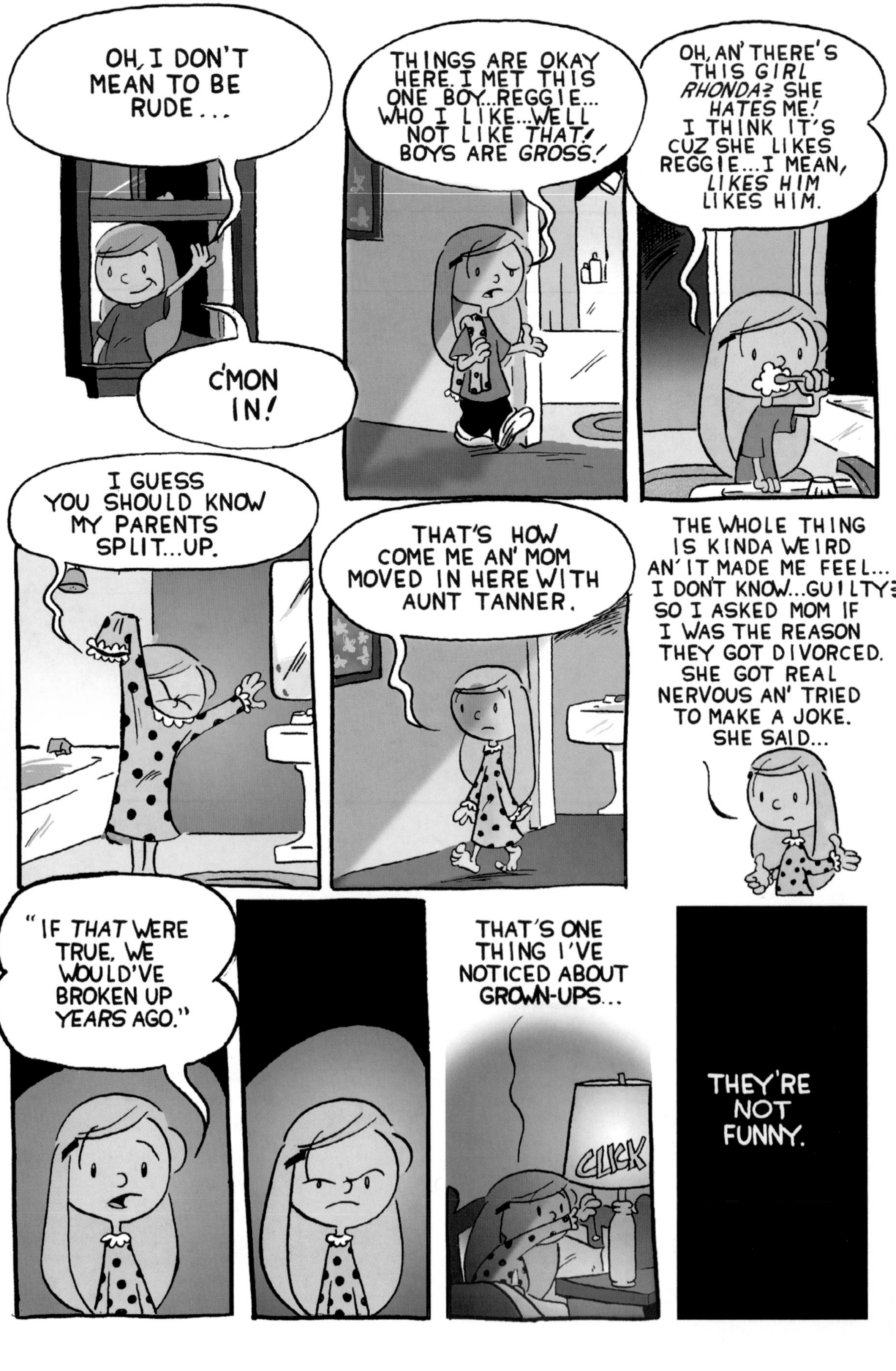
OH, I DON'T MEAN TO BE RUDE...
C'MON IN!
THINGS ARE OKAY HERE. I MET THIS ONE BOY...REGGIE... WHO I LIKE...WELL NOT LIKE THAT! BOYS ARE GROSS!
OH, AN' THERE'S THIS GIRL RHONDA? SHE HATES ME! I THINK IT'S CUZ SHE LIKES REGGIE...I MEAN, LIKES HIM LIKES HIM.
I GUESS YOU SHOULD KNOW MY PARENTS SPLIT...UP.
THAT'S HOW COME ME AN' MOM MOVED IN HERE WITH AUNT TANNER.
THE WHOLE THING IS KINDA WEIRD AN' IT MADE ME FEEL... I DON'T KNOW...GUILTY? SO I ASKED MOM IF I WAS THE REASON THEY GOT DIVORCED. SHE GOT REAL NERVOUS AN' TRIED TO MAKE A JOKE. SHE SAID...
"IF THAT WERE TRUE, WE WOULD'VE BROKEN UP YEARS AGO."
THAT'S ONE THING I'VE NOTICED ABOUT GROWN-UPS...
CLICK
THEY'RE NOT FUNNY.

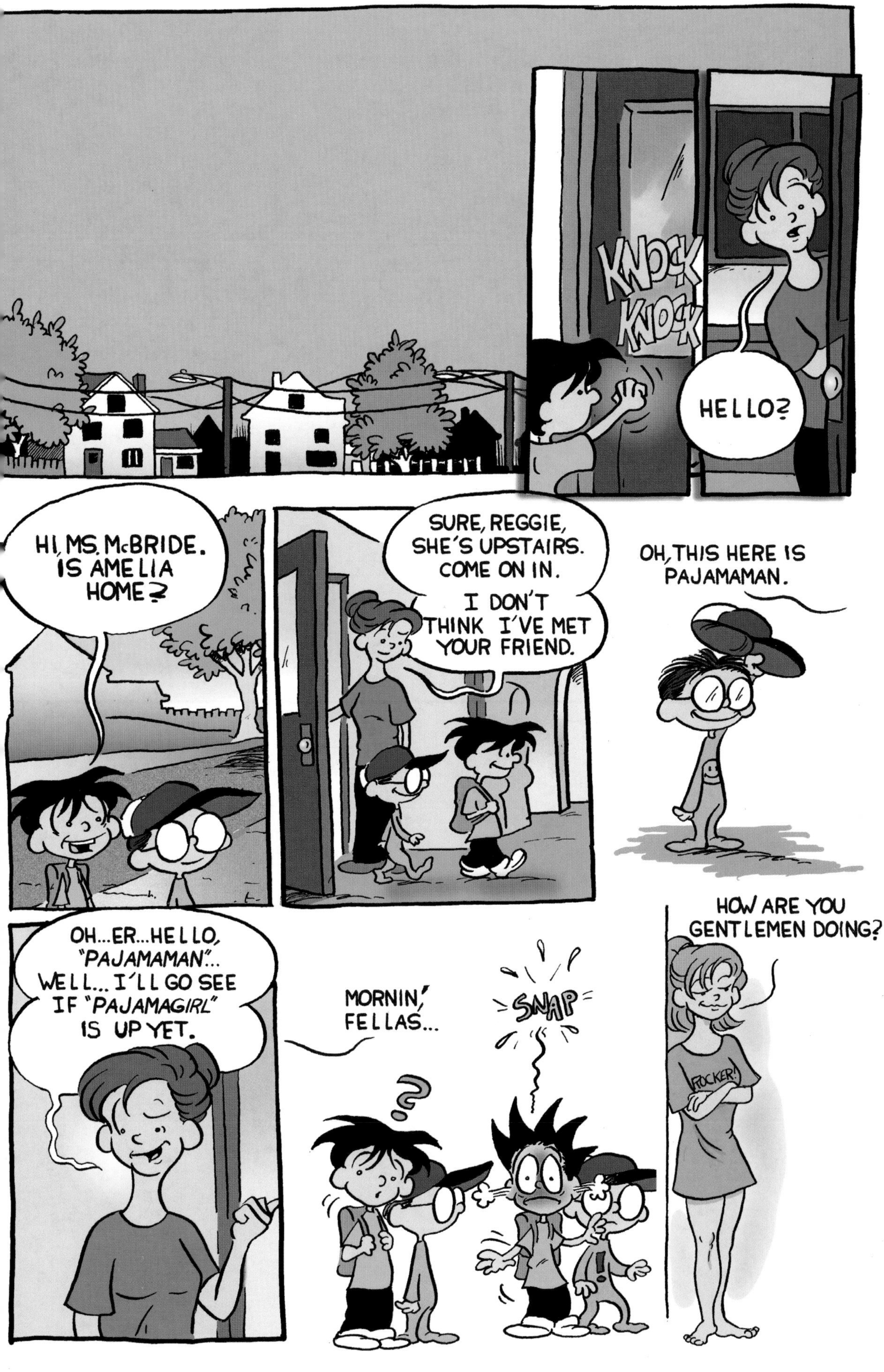
KNOCK KNOCK
HELLO?
HI, MS. McBRIDE. IS AMELIA HOME?
SURE, REGGIE, SHE'S UPSTAIRS. COME ON IN.
I DON'T THINK I'VE MET YOUR FRIEND.
OH, THIS HERE IS PAJAMAMAN.
OH...ER...HELLO, "PAJAMAMAN"... WELL... I'LL GO SEE IF "PAJAMAGIRL" IS UP YET.
MORNIN', FELLAS...
SNAP
HOW ARE YOU GENTLEMEN DOING?
ROCKER!

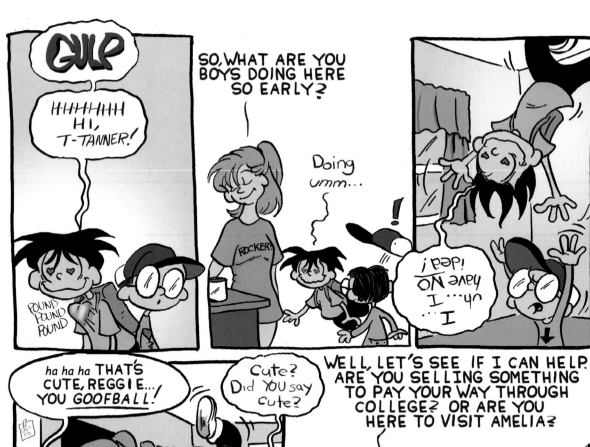

GULP

HHHHHHH HI, T-TANNER!

POUND POUND POUND

SO, WHAT ARE YOU BOYS DOING HERE SO EARLY?

Doing umm...

ROCKER

I...uh...I have NO idea!

ha ha ha THAT'S CUTE, REGGIE.../ YOU GOOFBALL!

MILK EGGS V. VALUNO CD

ROCKER

Cute? Did YOU say cute?

WELL, LET'S SEE IF I CAN HELP... ARE YOU SELLING SOMETHING TO PAY YOUR WAY THROUGH COLLEGE? OR ARE YOU HERE TO VISIT AMELIA?

umm...

THUD

Who's Amelia?

ROCK

AHEM!

CRASH!

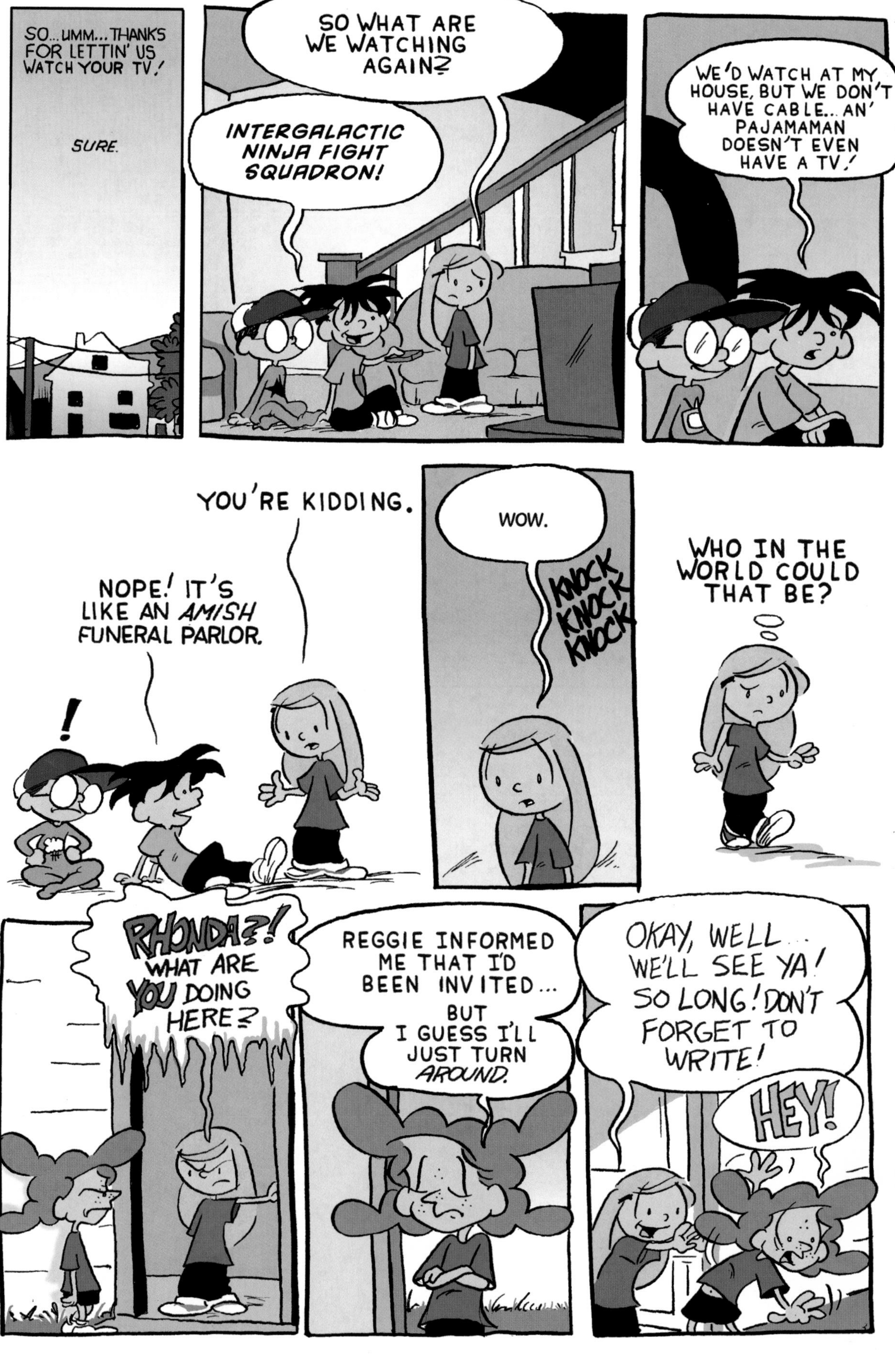
SO...UMM...THANKS FOR LETTIN' US WATCH YOUR TV!
SURE.
SO WHAT ARE WE WATCHING AGAIN?
INTERGALACTIC NINJA FIGHT SQUADRON!
WE'D WATCH AT MY HOUSE, BUT WE DON'T HAVE CABLE... AN' PAJAMAMAN DOESN'T EVEN HAVE A TV!
YOU'RE KIDDING.
NOPE! IT'S LIKE AN AMISH FUNERAL PARLOR.
!
WOW.
KNOCK KNOCK KNOCK
WHO IN THE WORLD COULD THAT BE?
RHONDA?! WHAT ARE YOU DOING HERE?
REGGIE INFORMED ME THAT I'D BEEN INVITED...
BUT I GUESS I'LL JUST TURN AROUND.
OKAY, WELL... WE'LL SEE YA! SO LONG! DON'T FORGET TO WRITE!
HEY!

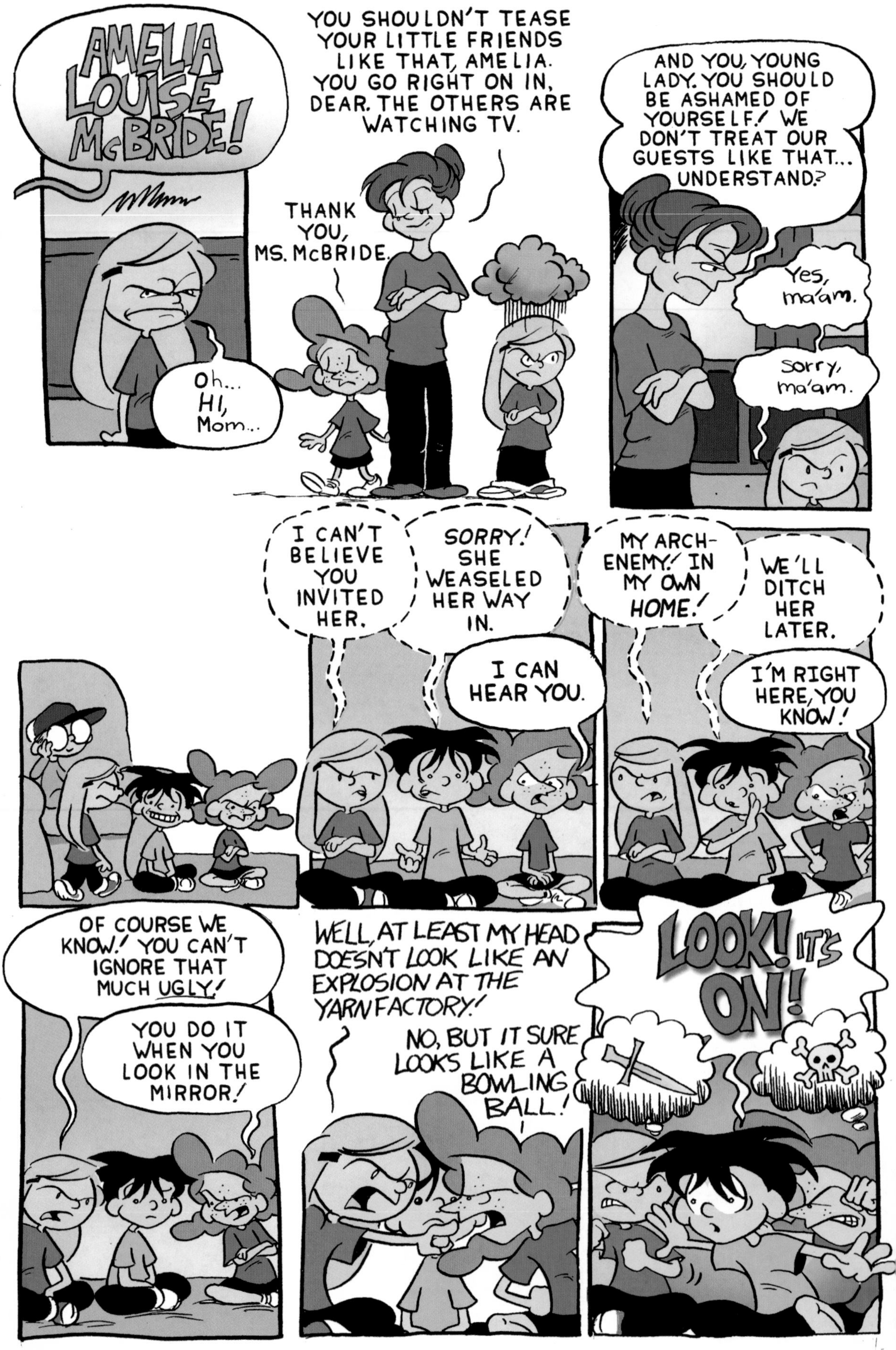
AMELIA LOUISE McBRIDE!
Oh... HI, Mom...
YOU SHOULDN'T TEASE YOUR LITTLE FRIENDS LIKE THAT, AMELIA. YOU GO RIGHT ON IN, DEAR. THE OTHERS ARE WATCHING TV.
THANK YOU, MS. McBRIDE.
AND YOU, YOUNG LADY. YOU SHOULD BE ASHAMED OF YOURSELF! WE DON'T TREAT OUR GUESTS LIKE THAT... UNDERSTAND?
Yes, ma'am.
Sorry, ma'am.
I CAN'T BELIEVE YOU INVITED HER.
SORRY! SHE WEASELED HER WAY IN.
I CAN HEAR YOU.
MY ARCH-ENEMY! IN MY OWN HOME!
WE'LL DITCH HER LATER.
I'M RIGHT HERE, YOU KNOW!
OF COURSE WE KNOW! YOU CAN'T IGNORE THAT MUCH UGLY!
YOU DO IT WHEN YOU LOOK IN THE MIRROR!
WELL, AT LEAST MY HEAD DOESN'T LOOK LIKE AN EXPLOSION AT THE YARN FACTORY!
NO, BUT IT SURE LOOKS LIKE A BOWLING BALL!
LOOK! IT'S ON!

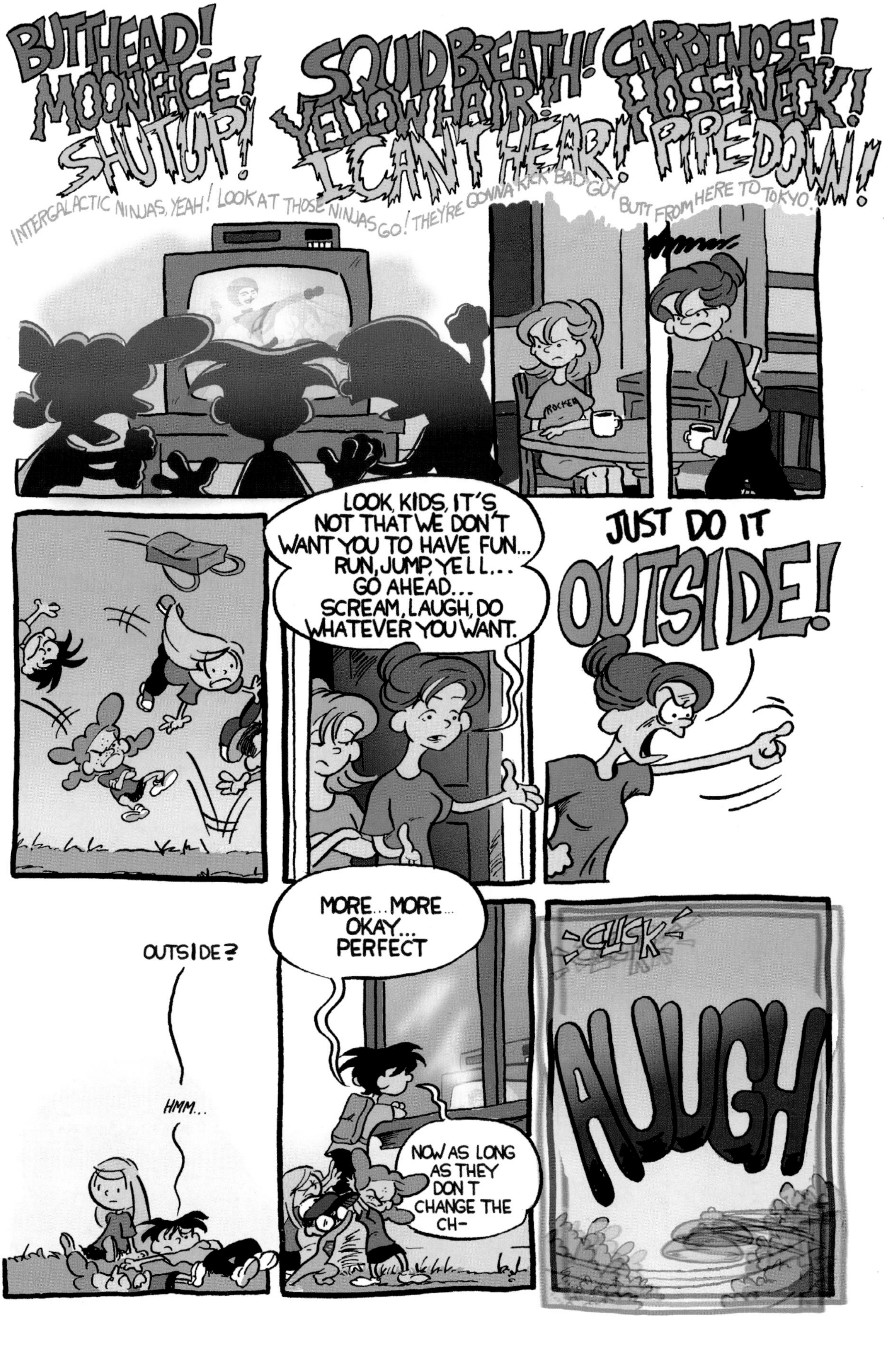
BUTTHEAD! MOONFACE! SHUTUP! SQUIDBREATH! YELLOWHAIR! I CAN'T HEAR! CARROTNOSE! HOSENECK! PIPE DOWN!
INTERGALACTIC NINJAS, YEAH! LOOK AT THOSE NINJAS GO! THEY'RE GONNA 'KICK' BAD GUY BUTT FROM HERE TO TOKYO!
LOOK, KIDS, IT'S NOT THAT WE DON'T WANT YOU TO HAVE FUN... RUN, JUMP, YELL... GO AHEAD... SCREAM, LAUGH, DO WHATEVER YOU WANT.
JUST DO IT OUTSIDE!
OUTSIDE?
HMM...
MORE... MORE... OKAY... PERFECT
NOW AS LONG AS THEY DON'T CHANGE THE CH-
CLICK
AUUGH!

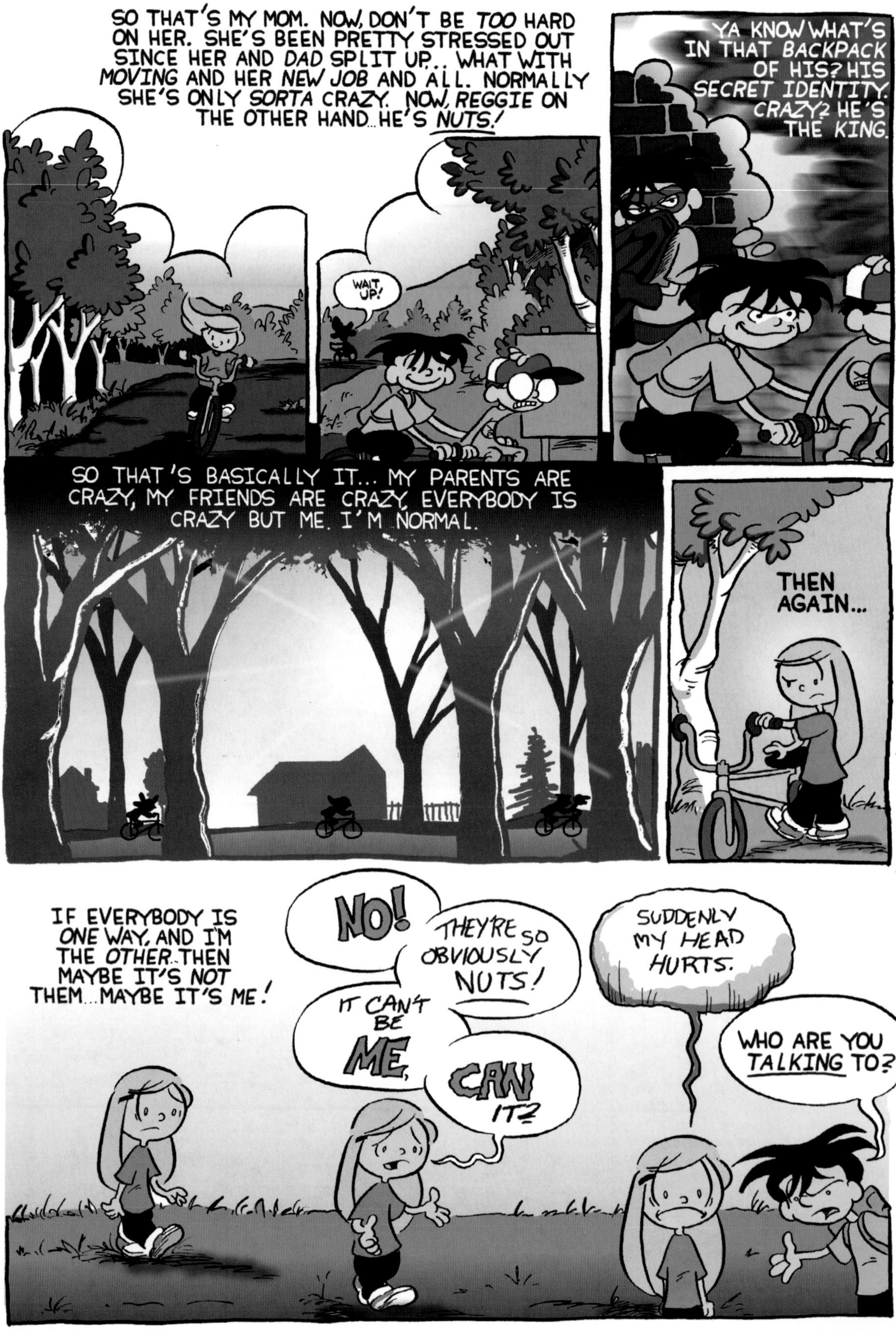
SO THAT'S MY MOM. NOW, DON'T BE TOO HARD ON HER. SHE'S BEEN PRETTY STRESSED OUT SINCE HER AND DAD SPLIT UP... WHAT WITH MOVING AND HER NEW JOB AND ALL. NORMALLY SHE'S ONLY SORTA CRAZY. NOW, REGGIE ON THE OTHER HAND... HE'S NUTS!
WAIT UP!
YA KNOW WHAT'S IN THAT BACKPACK OF HIS? HIS SECRET IDENTITY. CRAZY? HE'S THE KING.
SO THAT'S BASICALLY IT... MY PARENTS ARE CRAZY, MY FRIENDS ARE CRAZY, EVERYBODY IS CRAZY BUT ME. I'M NORMAL.
THEN AGAIN...
IF EVERYBODY IS ONE WAY, AND I'M THE OTHER... THEN MAYBE IT'S NOT THEM... MAYBE IT'S ME!
NO!
THEY'RE SO OBVIOUSLY NUTS!
IT CAN'T BE ME,
CAN IT?
SUDDENLY MY HEAD HURTS.
WHO ARE YOU TALKING TO?

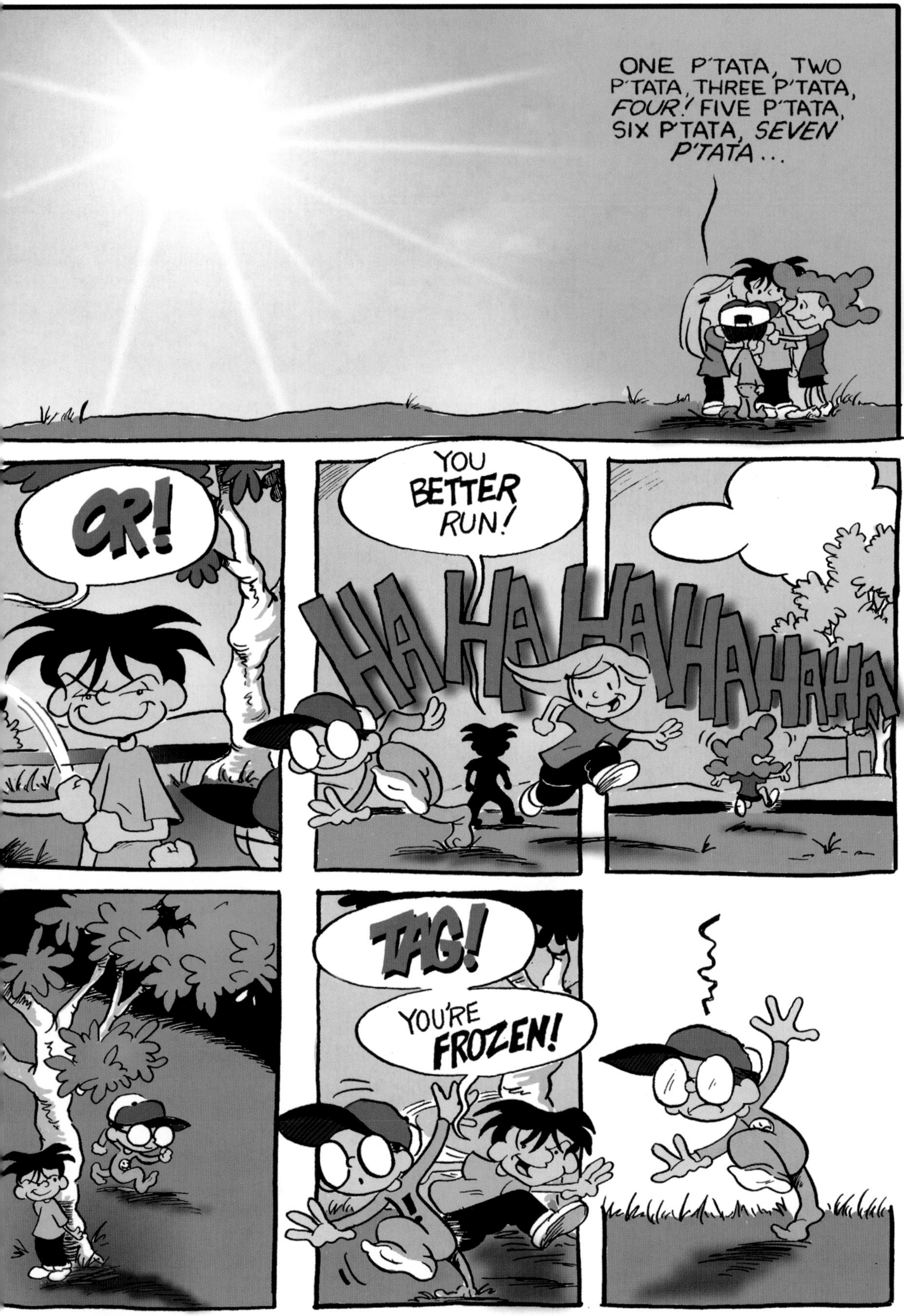

ONE P'TATA, TWO P'TATA, THREE P'TATA, *FOUR!* FIVE P'TATA, SIX P'TATA, *SEVEN* P'TATA...
OR!
YOU BETTER RUN!
HA HA HA HA HA HA HA
TAG!
YOU'RE FROZEN!

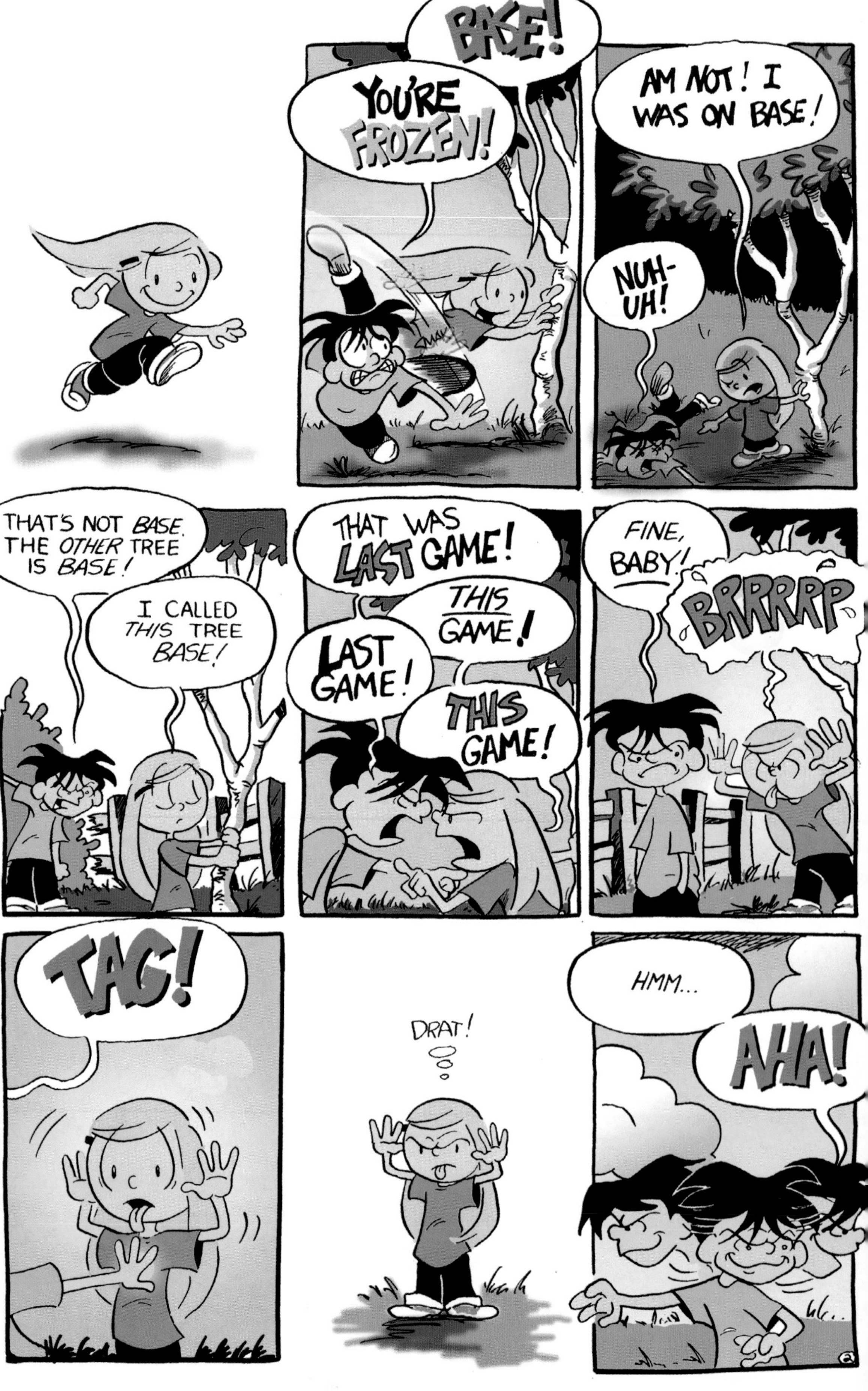
BASE!
YOU'RE FROZEN!
AM NOT! I WAS ON BASE!
NUH-UH!
THAT'S NOT BASE. THE OTHER TREE IS BASE!
I CALLED THIS TREE BASE!
THAT WAS LAST GAME!
THIS GAME!
LAST GAME!
THIS GAME!
FINE, BABY!
BRRRRP
TAG!
DRAT!
HMM...
AHA!

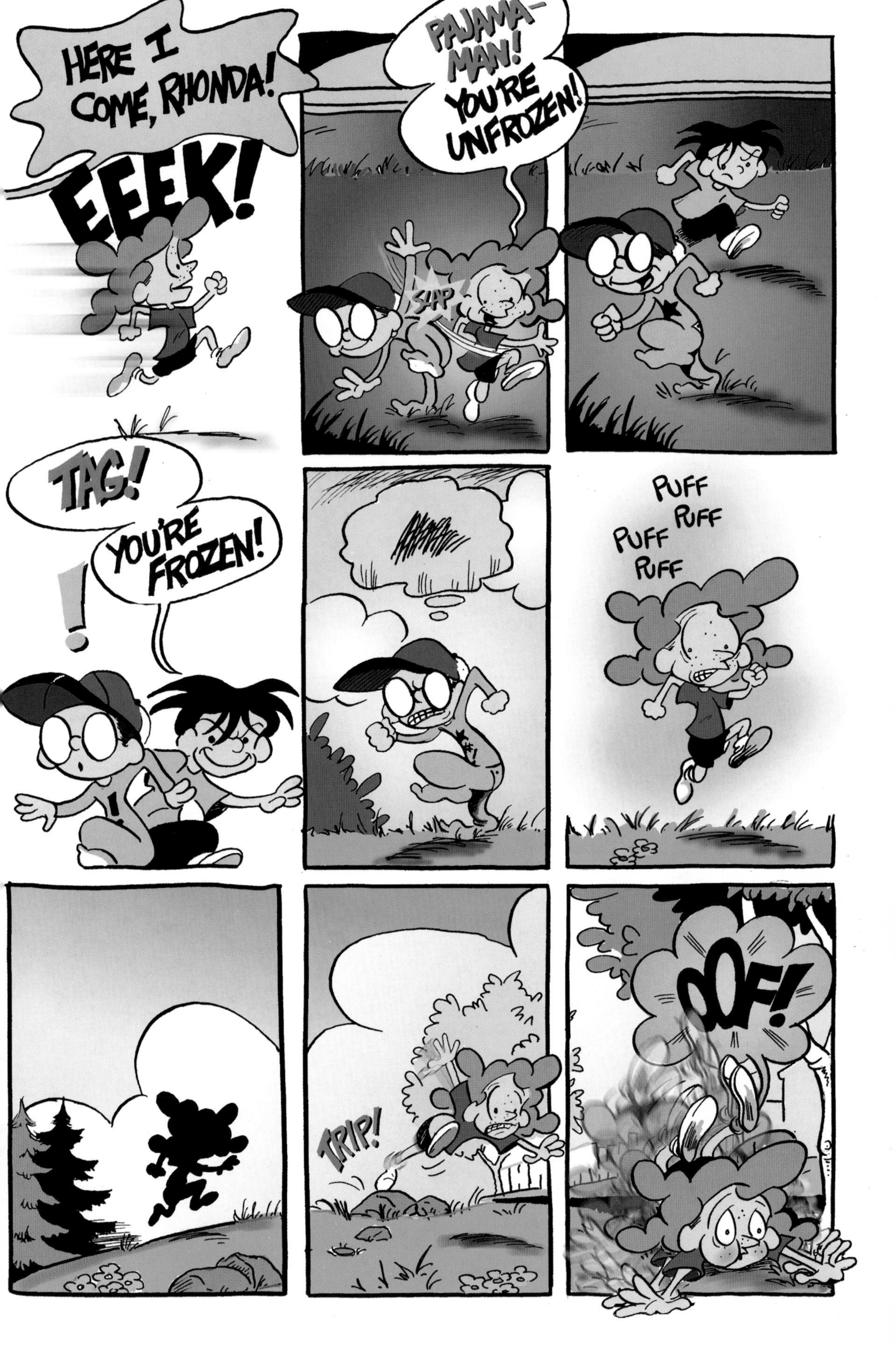
HERE I COME, RHONDA!
EEEK!
PAJAMA-MAN! YOU'RE UNFROZEN!
SLAP
TAG!
YOU'RE FROZEN!
!
PUFF PUFF PUFF PUFF
TRIP!
OOF!

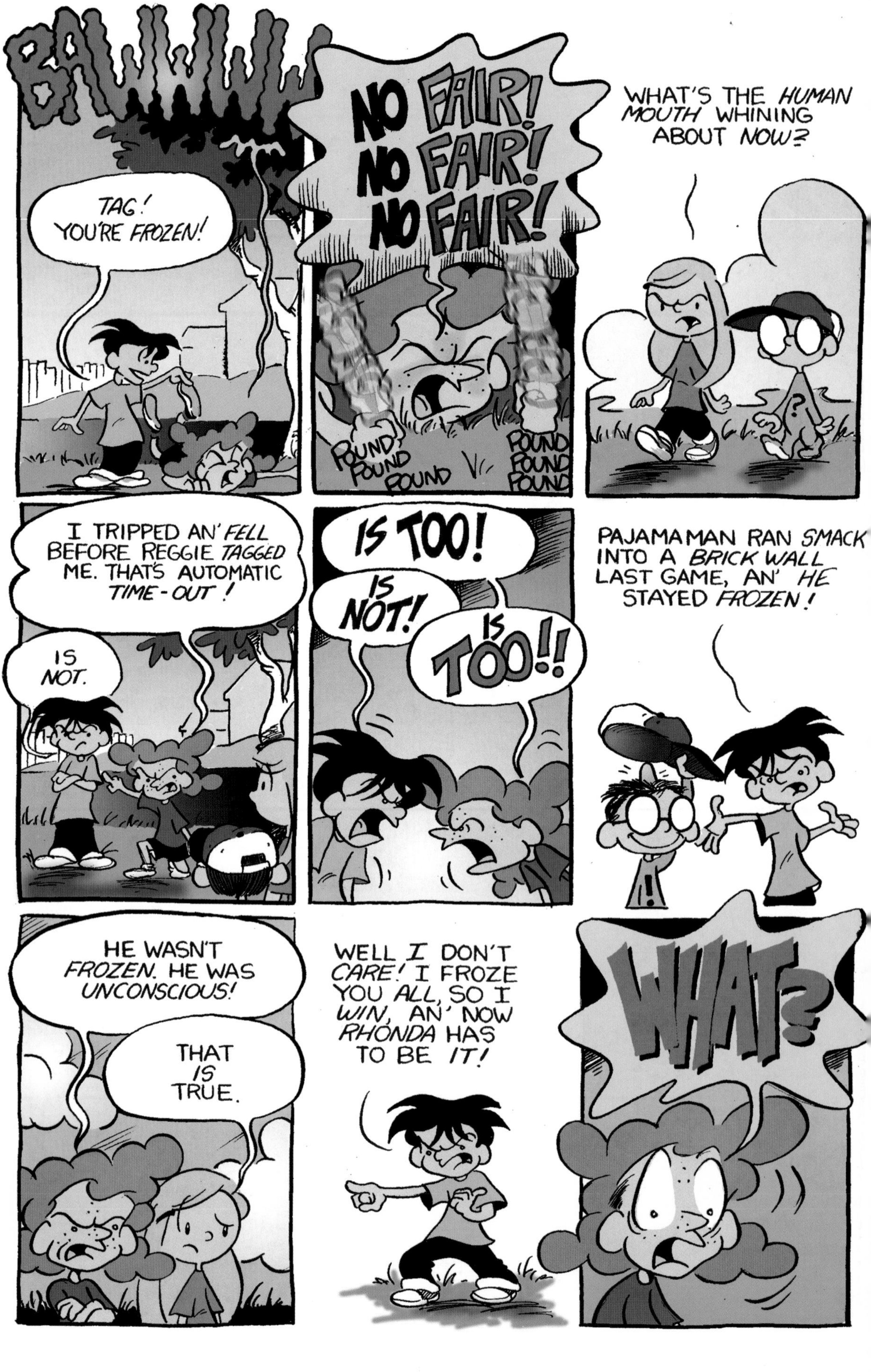
BAWWW
TAG! YOU'RE FROZEN!
NO FAIR! NO FAIR! NO FAIR!
POUND POUND POUND
POUND POUND POUND
WHAT'S THE HUMAN MOUTH WHINING ABOUT NOW?
I TRIPPED AN' FELL BEFORE REGGIE TAGGED ME. THAT'S AUTOMATIC TIME-OUT!
IS NOT.
IS TOO!
IS NOT!
IS TOO!!
PAJAMAMAN RAN SMACK INTO A BRICK WALL LAST GAME, AN' HE STAYED FROZEN!
HE WASN'T FROZEN. HE WAS UNCONSCIOUS!
THAT IS TRUE.
WELL I DON'T CARE! I FROZE YOU ALL, SO I WIN, AN' NOW RHONDA HAS TO BE IT!
WHAT?

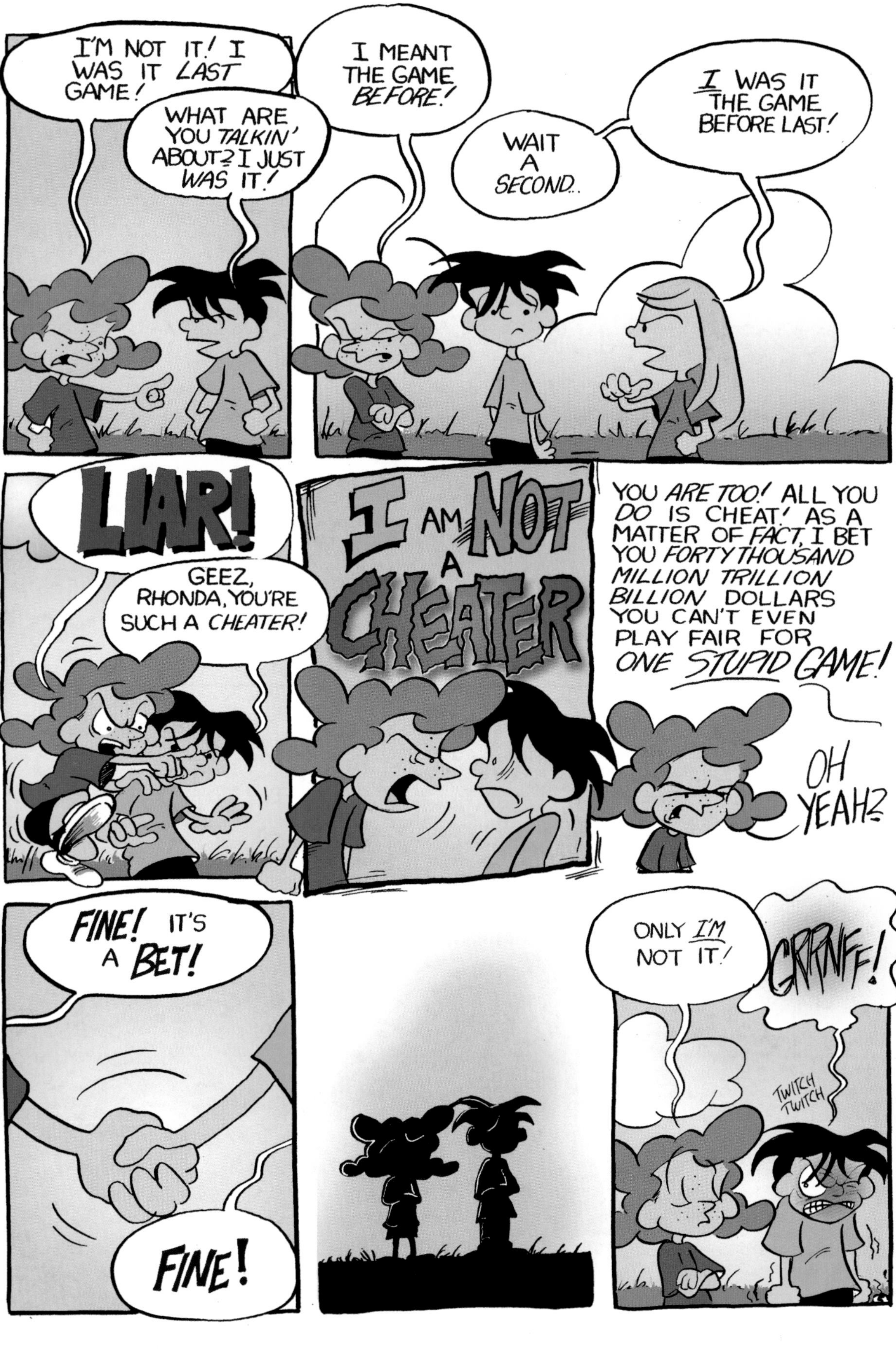

I'M NOT IT! I WAS IT LAST GAME!
WHAT ARE YOU TALKIN' ABOUT? I JUST WAS IT!
I MEANT THE GAME BEFORE!
WAIT A SECOND...
I WAS IT THE GAME BEFORE LAST!
LIAR!
GEEZ, RHONDA, YOU'RE SUCH A CHEATER!
I AM NOT A CHEATER
YOU ARE TOO! ALL YOU DO IS CHEAT! AS A MATTER OF FACT, I BET YOU FORTY THOUSAND MILLION TRILLION BILLION DOLLARS YOU CAN'T EVEN PLAY FAIR FOR ONE STUPID GAME!
OH YEAH?
FINE! IT'S A BET!
FINE!
ONLY I'M NOT IT!
GRRNFF!
TWITCH TWITCH

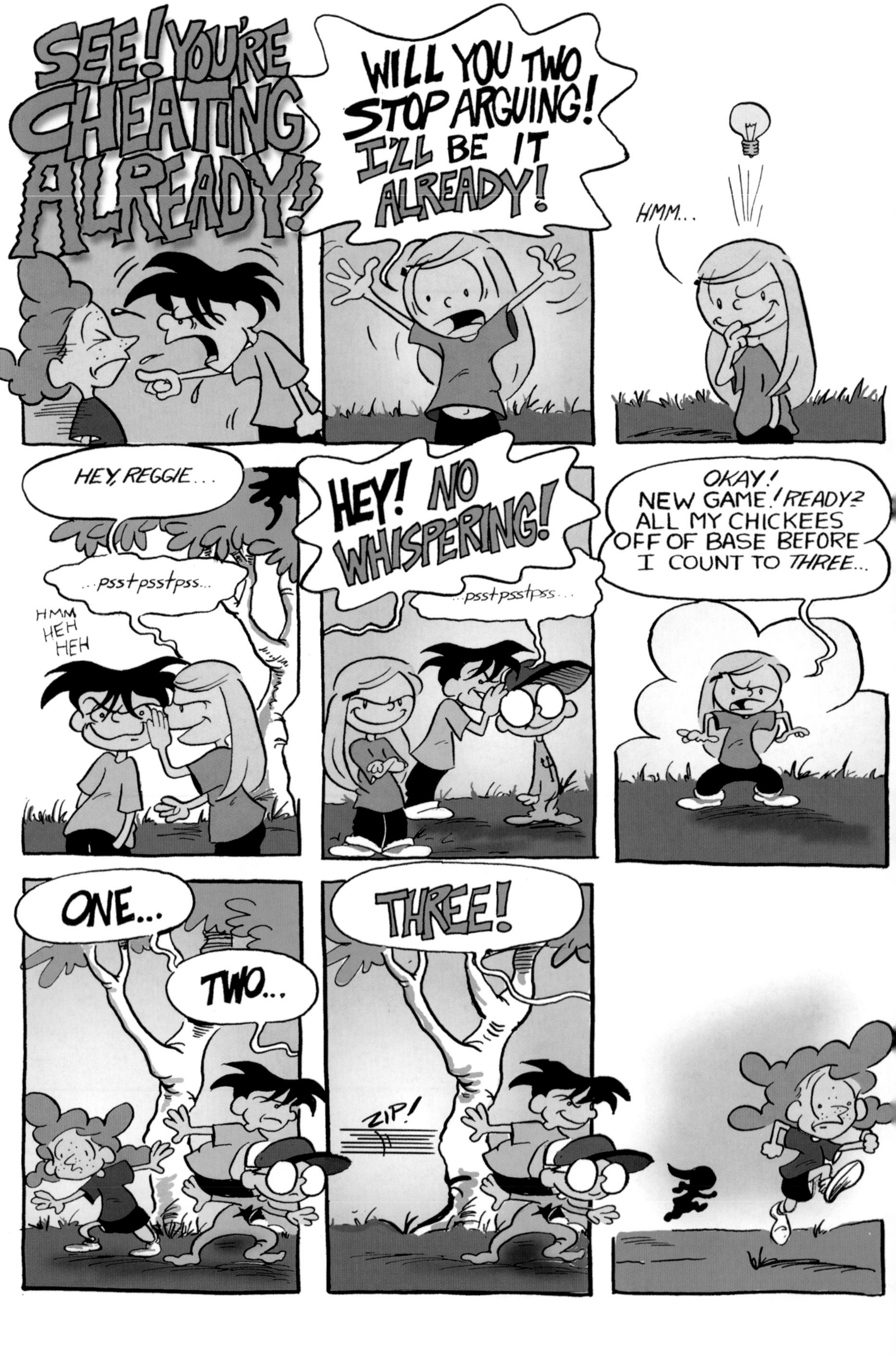
SEE! YOU'RE CHEATING ALREADY!
WILL YOU TWO STOP ARGUING! I'LL BE IT ALREADY!
HMM...
HEY, REGGIE...
...psstpsstpss...
HMM HEH HEH
HEY! NO WHISPERING!
...psstpsstpss...
OKAY! NEW GAME! READY? ALL MY CHICKEES OFF OF BASE BEFORE I COUNT TO THREE...
ONE...
TWO...
THREE!
ZIP!

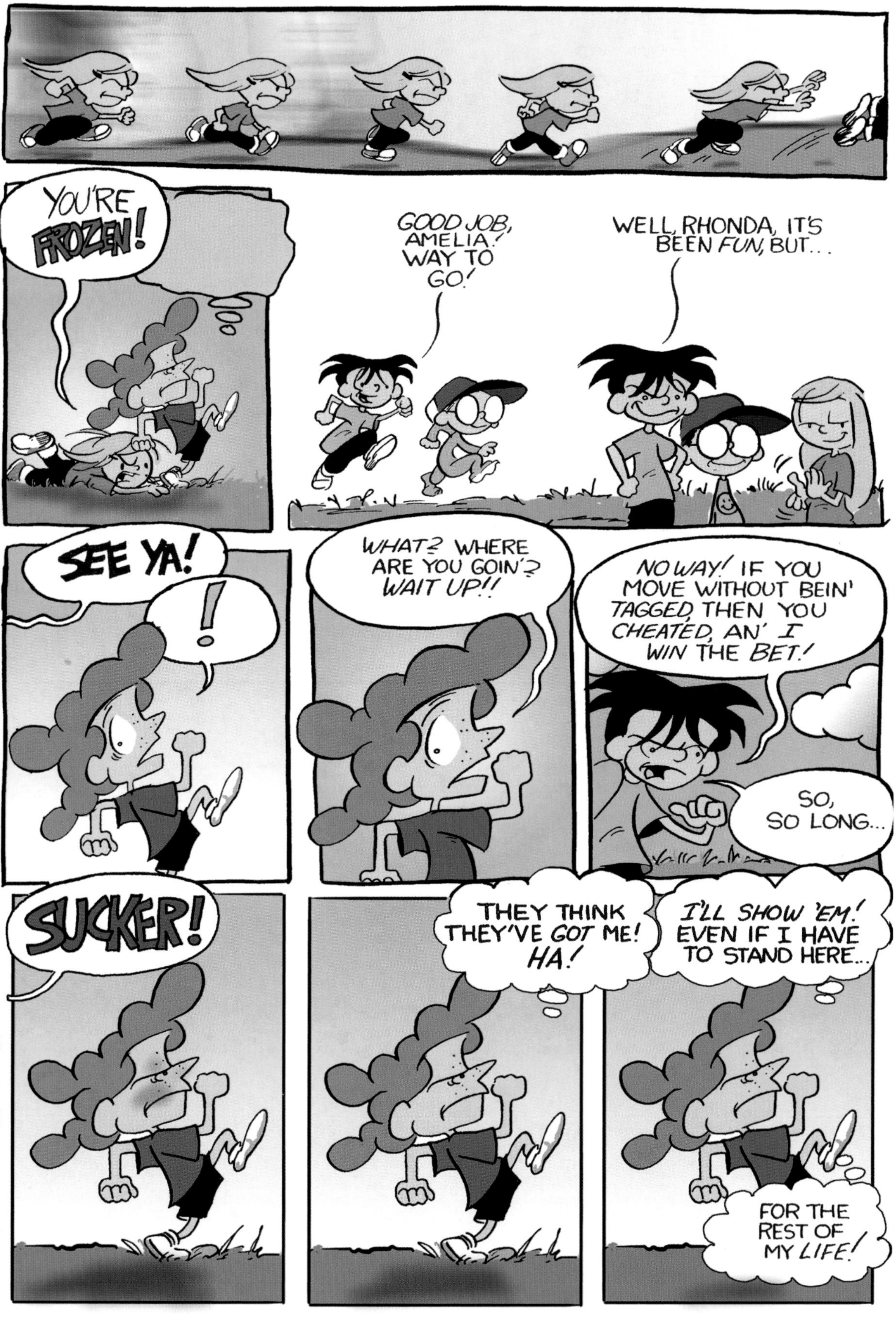
YOU'RE FROZEN!
GOOD JOB, AMELIA! WAY TO GO!
WELL, RHONDA, IT'S BEEN FUN, BUT...
SEE YA!
!
WHAT? WHERE ARE YOU GOIN'? WAIT UP!!
NO WAY! IF YOU MOVE WITHOUT BEIN' TAGGED, THEN YOU CHEATED, AN' I WIN THE BET!
SO, SO LONG...
SUCKER!
THEY THINK THEY'VE GOT ME! HA!
I'LL SHOW 'EM! EVEN IF I HAVE TO STAND HERE...
FOR THE REST OF MY LIFE!

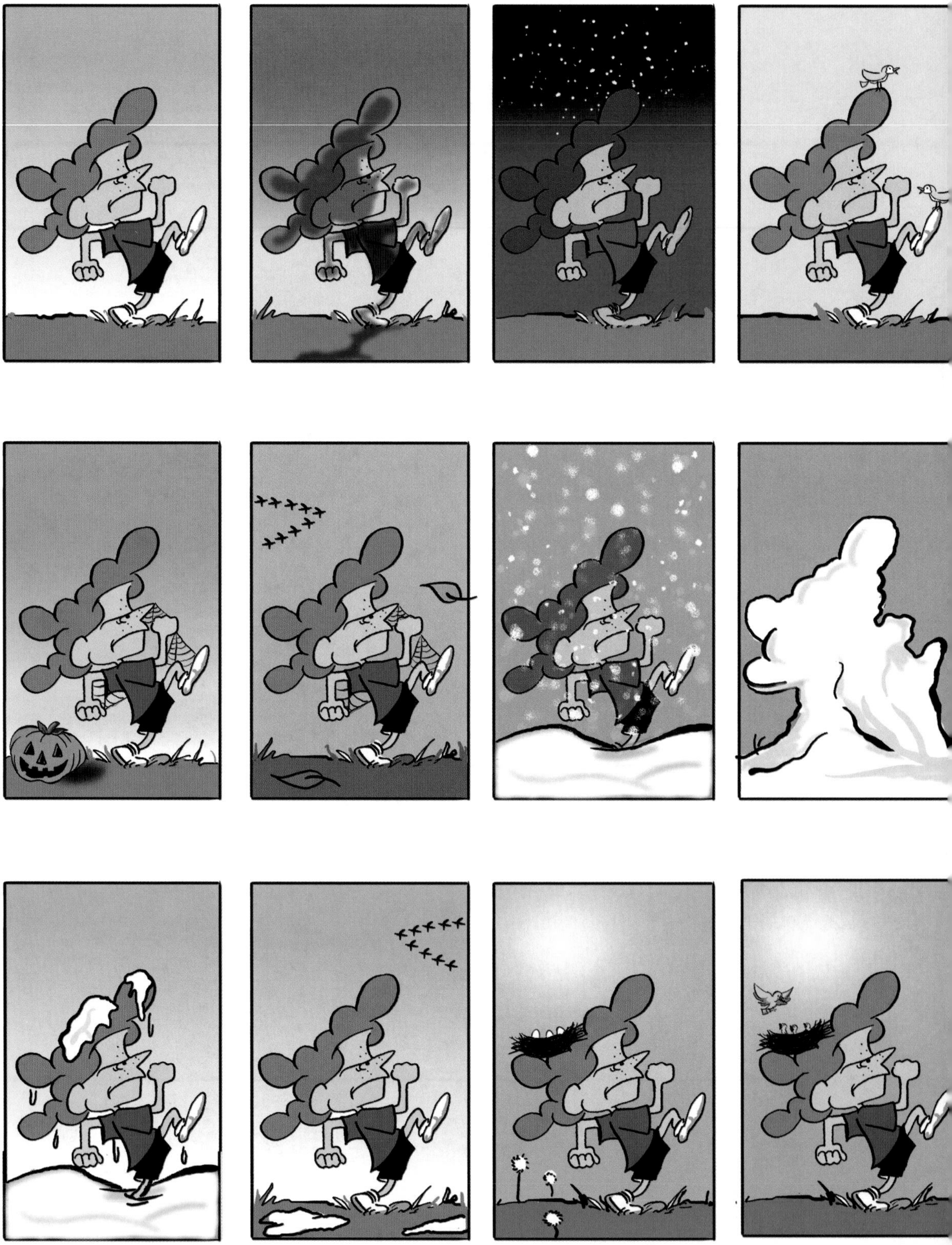

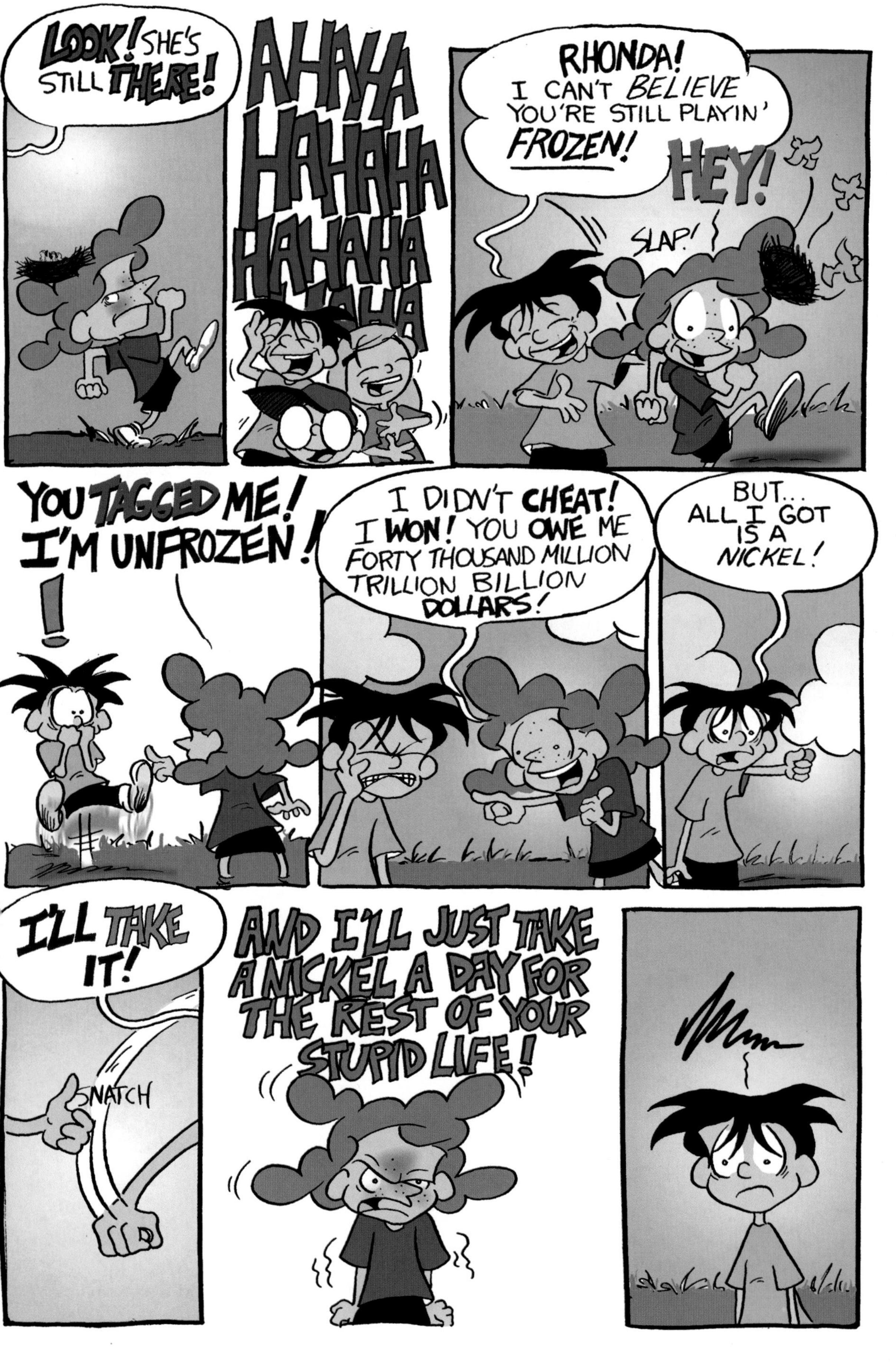

LOOK! SHE'S STILL THERE!
AHAHA HAHAHA HAHAHA HAHA
RHONDA! I CAN'T BELIEVE YOU'RE STILL PLAYIN' FROZEN!
HEY!
SLAP!
YOU TAGGED ME! I'M UNFROZEN!
!
I DIDN'T CHEAT! I WON! YOU OWE ME FORTY THOUSAND MILLION TRILLION BILLION DOLLARS!
BUT... ALL I GOT IS A NICKEL!
I'LL TAKE IT!
SNATCH
AND I'LL JUST TAKE A NICKEL A DAY FOR THE REST OF YOUR STUPID LIFE!

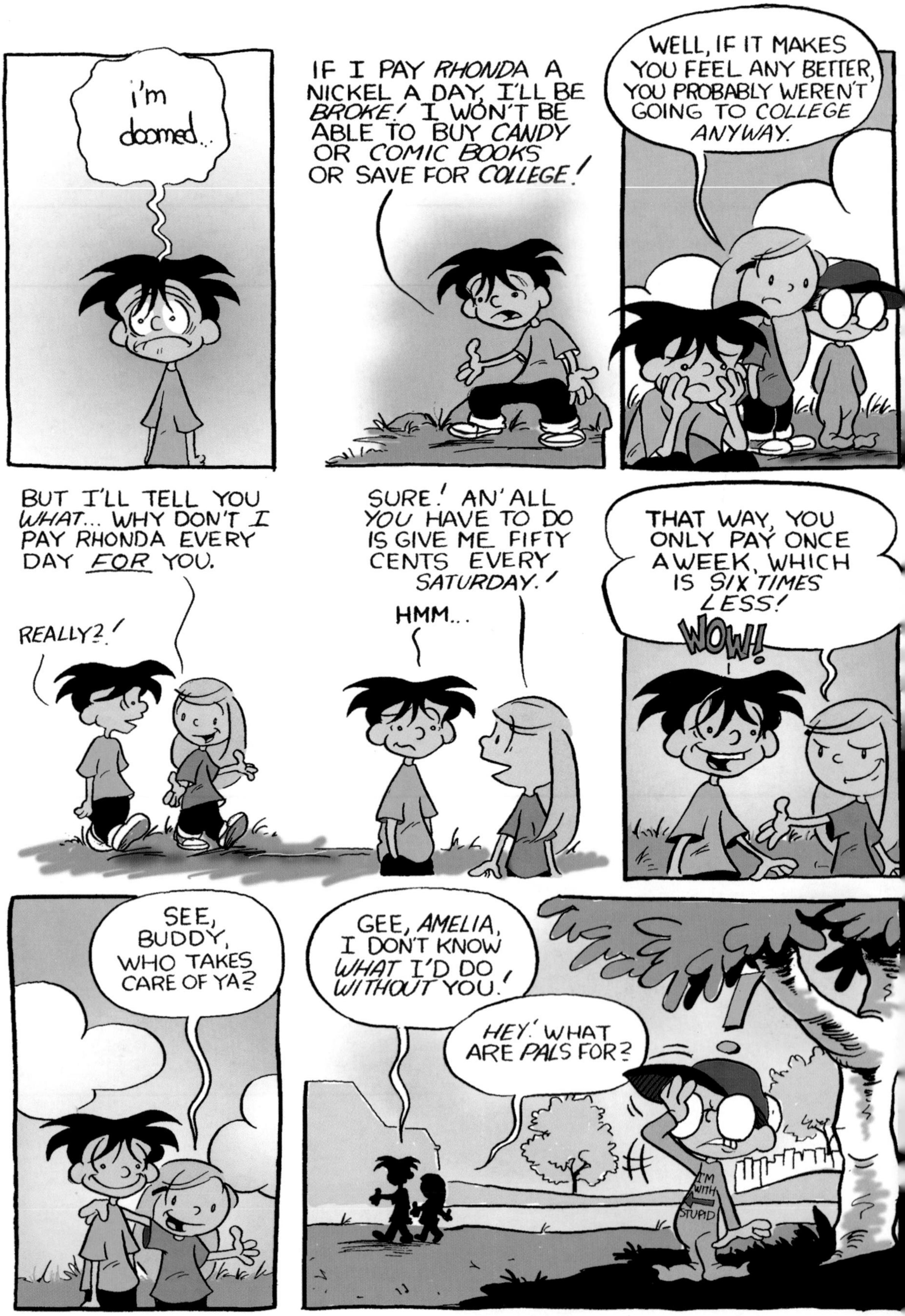

i'm doomed...
IF I PAY RHONDA A NICKEL A DAY, I'LL BE BROKE! I WON'T BE ABLE TO BUY CANDY OR COMIC BOOKS OR SAVE FOR COLLEGE!
WELL, IF IT MAKES YOU FEEL ANY BETTER, YOU PROBABLY WEREN'T GOING TO COLLEGE ANYWAY.
BUT I'LL TELL YOU WHAT... WHY DON'T I PAY RHONDA EVERY DAY FOR YOU.
REALLY?!
SURE! AN' ALL YOU HAVE TO DO IS GIVE ME FIFTY CENTS EVERY SATURDAY!
HMM...
THAT WAY, YOU ONLY PAY ONCE A WEEK, WHICH IS SIX TIMES LESS!
WOW!
SEE, BUDDY, WHO TAKES CARE OF YA?
GEE, AMELIA, I DON'T KNOW WHAT I'D DO WITHOUT YOU!
HEY! WHAT ARE PALS FOR?
I'M WITH STUPID

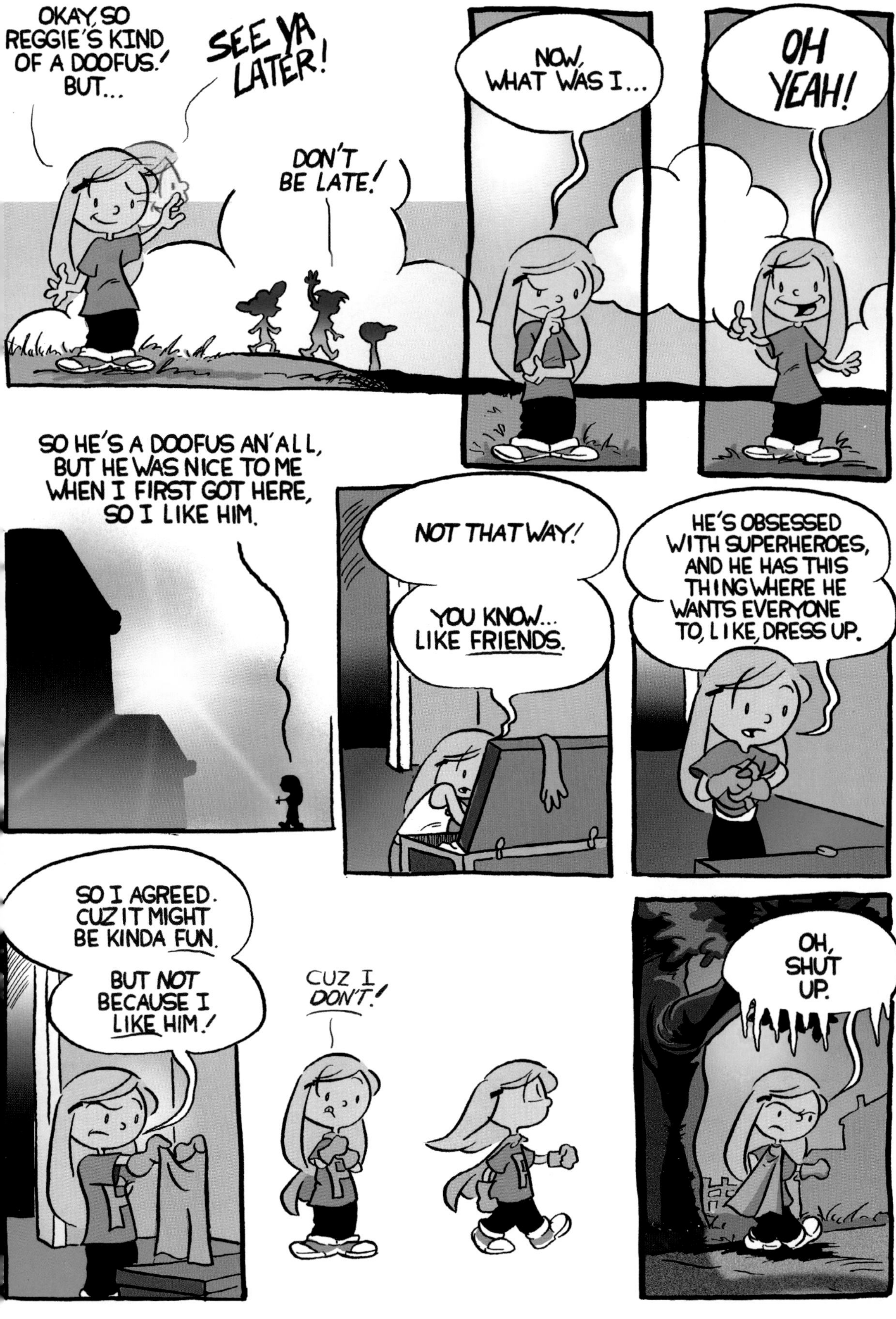

OKAY, SO REGGIE'S KIND OF A DOOFUS! BUT...
SEE YA LATER!
DON'T BE LATE!
NOW, WHAT WAS I...
OH YEAH!
SO HE'S A DOOFUS AN' ALL, BUT HE WAS NICE TO ME WHEN I FIRST GOT HERE, SO I LIKE HIM.
NOT THAT WAY!
YOU KNOW... LIKE FRIENDS.
HE'S OBSESSED WITH SUPERHEROES, AND HE HAS THIS THING WHERE HE WANTS EVERYONE TO, LIKE, DRESS UP.
SO I AGREED. CUZ IT MIGHT BE KINDA FUN.
BUT NOT BECAUSE I LIKE HIM!
CUZ I DON'T!
OH, SHUT UP.

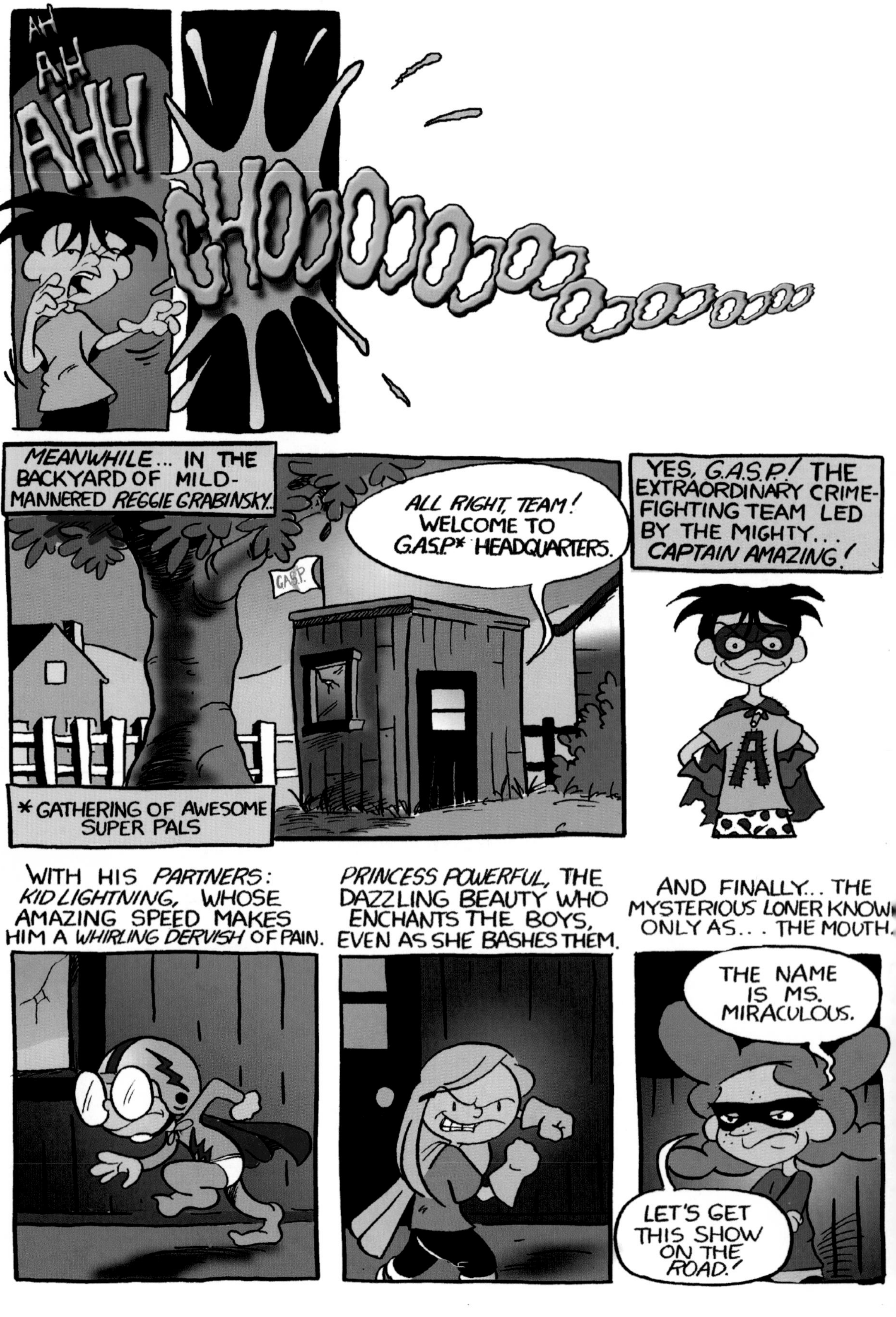
AH AH AHH
CHOOOOOOOOOOOOOOOOOO
MEANWHILE... IN THE BACKYARD OF MILD-MANNERED REGGIE GRABINSKY...
ALL RIGHT, TEAM! WELCOME TO G.A.S.P.* HEADQUARTERS.
G.A.S.P.
* GATHERING OF AWESOME SUPER PALS
YES, G.A.S.P.! THE EXTRAORDINARY CRIME-FIGHTING TEAM LED BY THE MIGHTY... CAPTAIN AMAZING!
A
WITH HIS PARTNERS: KID LIGHTNING, WHOSE AMAZING SPEED MAKES HIM A WHIRLING DERVISH OF PAIN.
PRINCESS POWERFUL, THE DAZZLING BEAUTY WHO ENCHANTS THE BOYS, EVEN AS SHE BASHES THEM.
AND FINALLY... THE MYSTERIOUS LONER KNOWN ONLY AS... THE MOUTH.
THE NAME IS MS. MIRACULOUS.
LET'S GET THIS SHOW ON THE ROAD!

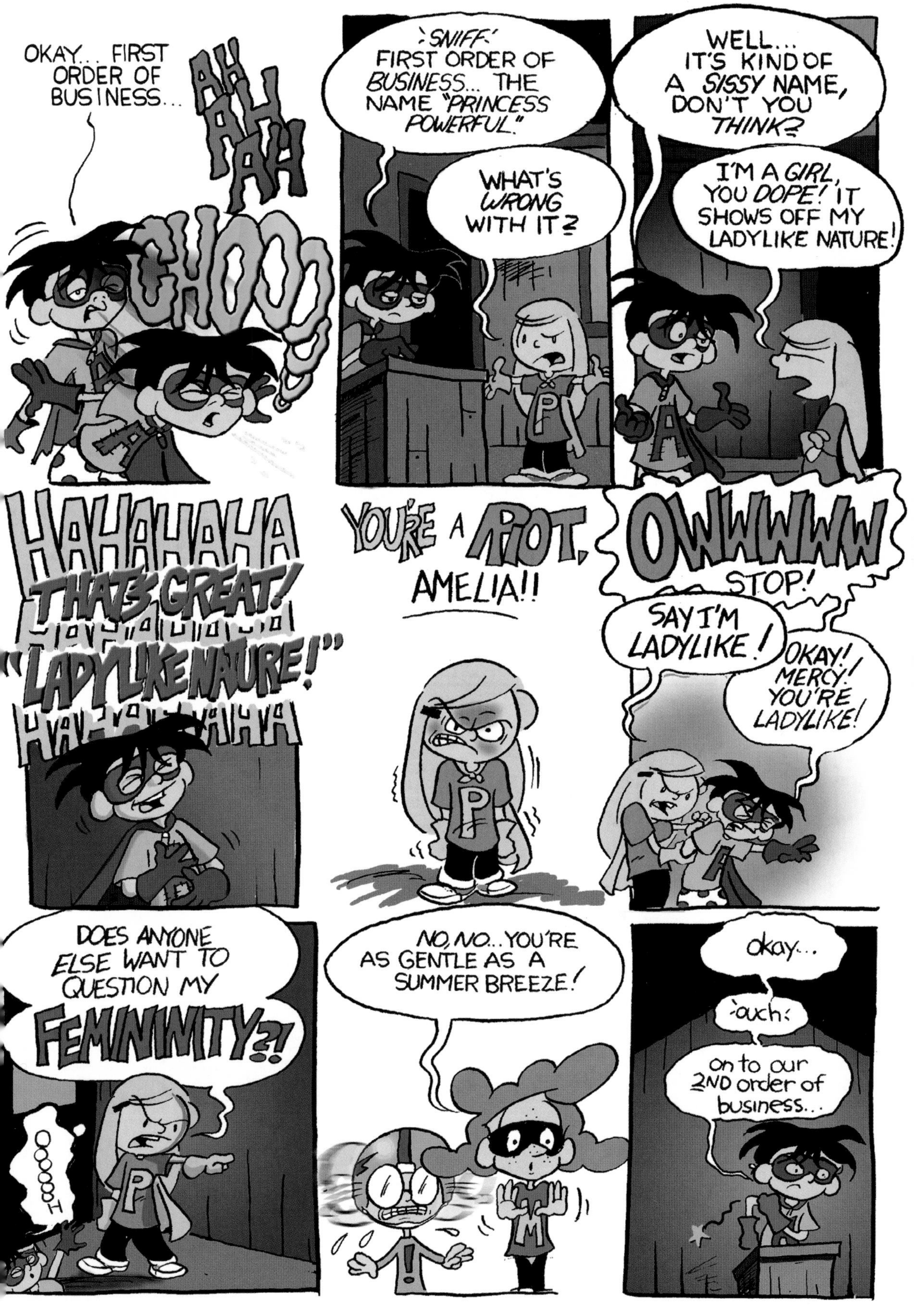
OKAY... FIRST ORDER OF BUSINESS...
AH AH AH AH
CHOOO
:SNIFF: FIRST ORDER OF BUSINESS... THE NAME "PRINCESS POWERFUL."
WHAT'S WRONG WITH IT?
WELL... IT'S KIND OF A SISSY NAME, DON'T YOU THINK?
I'M A GIRL, YOU DOPE! IT SHOWS OFF MY LADYLIKE NATURE!
HAHAHAHA
THAT'S GREAT!
"LADYLIKE NATURE!"
YOU'RE A RIOT, AMELIA!!
OWWWWW
STOP!
SAY I'M LADYLIKE!
OKAY! MERCY! YOU'RE LADYLIKE!
DOES ANYONE ELSE WANT TO QUESTION MY FEMININITY?!
OOOOOH
NO, NO... YOU'RE AS GENTLE AS A SUMMER BREEZE!
okay...
:ouch:
on to our 2ND order of business...

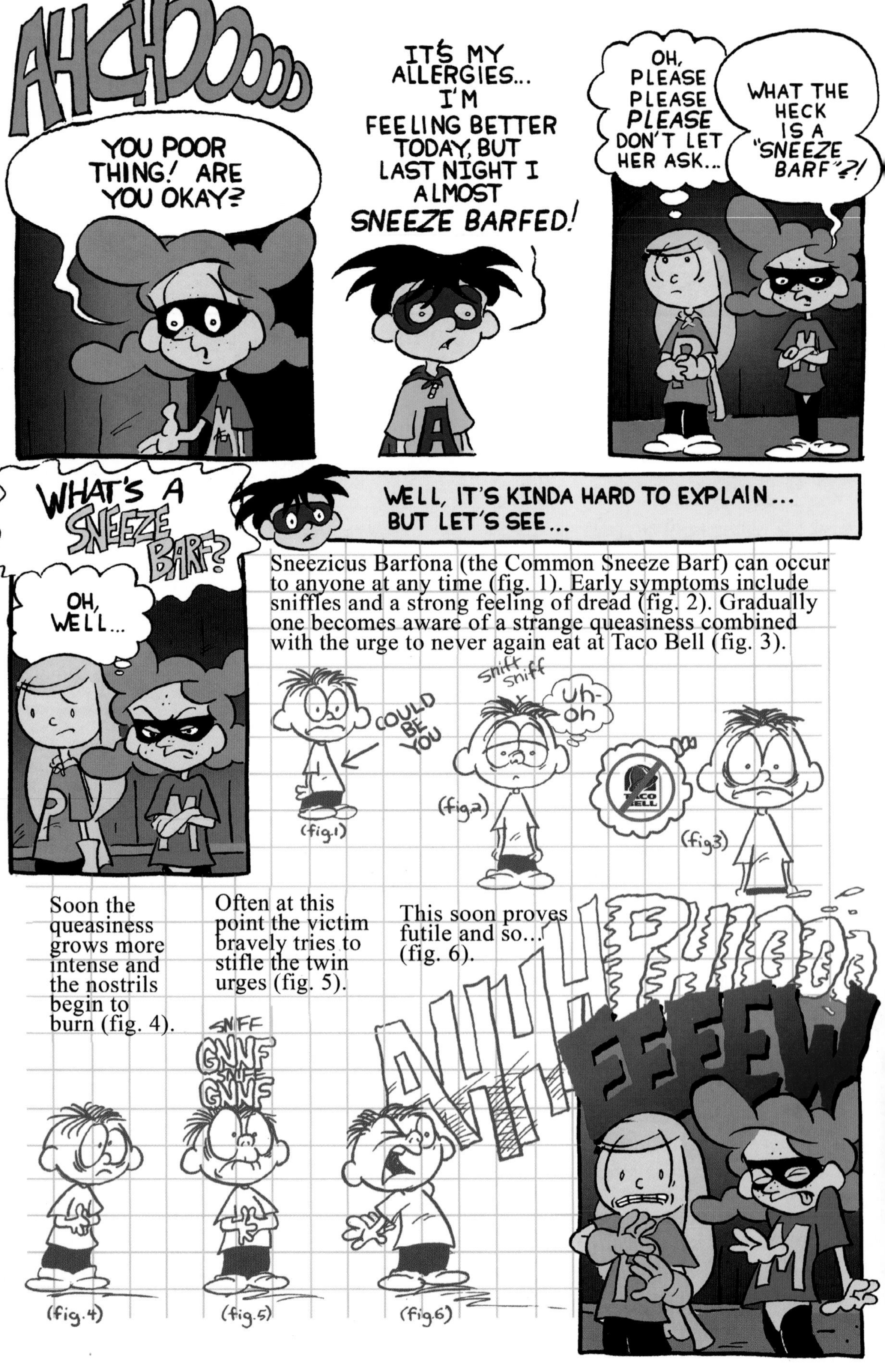
AHCHOOOOO
YOU POOR THING! ARE YOU OKAY?
IT'S MY ALLERGIES... I'M FEELING BETTER TODAY, BUT LAST NIGHT I ALMOST SNEEZE BARFED!
OH, PLEASE PLEASE PLEASE DON'T LET HER ASK...
WHAT THE HECK IS A "SNEEZE BARF"?!
WHAT'S A SNEEZE BARF?
OH, WELL...
WELL, IT'S KINDA HARD TO EXPLAIN... BUT LET'S SEE...
Sneezicus Barfona (the Common Sneeze Barf) can occur to anyone at any time (fig. 1). Early symptoms include sniffles and a strong feeling of dread (fig. 2). Gradually one becomes aware of a strange queasiness combined with the urge to never again eat at Taco Bell (fig. 3).
COULD BE YOU
(fig.1)
sniff sniff
uh-oh
(fig.2)
TACO BELL
(fig.3)
Soon the queasiness grows more intense and the nostrils begin to burn (fig. 4).
Often at this point the victim bravely tries to stifle the twin urges (fig. 5).
This soon proves futile and so... (fig. 6).
SNIFF
GNNF
SNIFF
GNNF
AHHHPUHOOO
EEEEW
(fig.4)
(fig.5)
(fig.6)

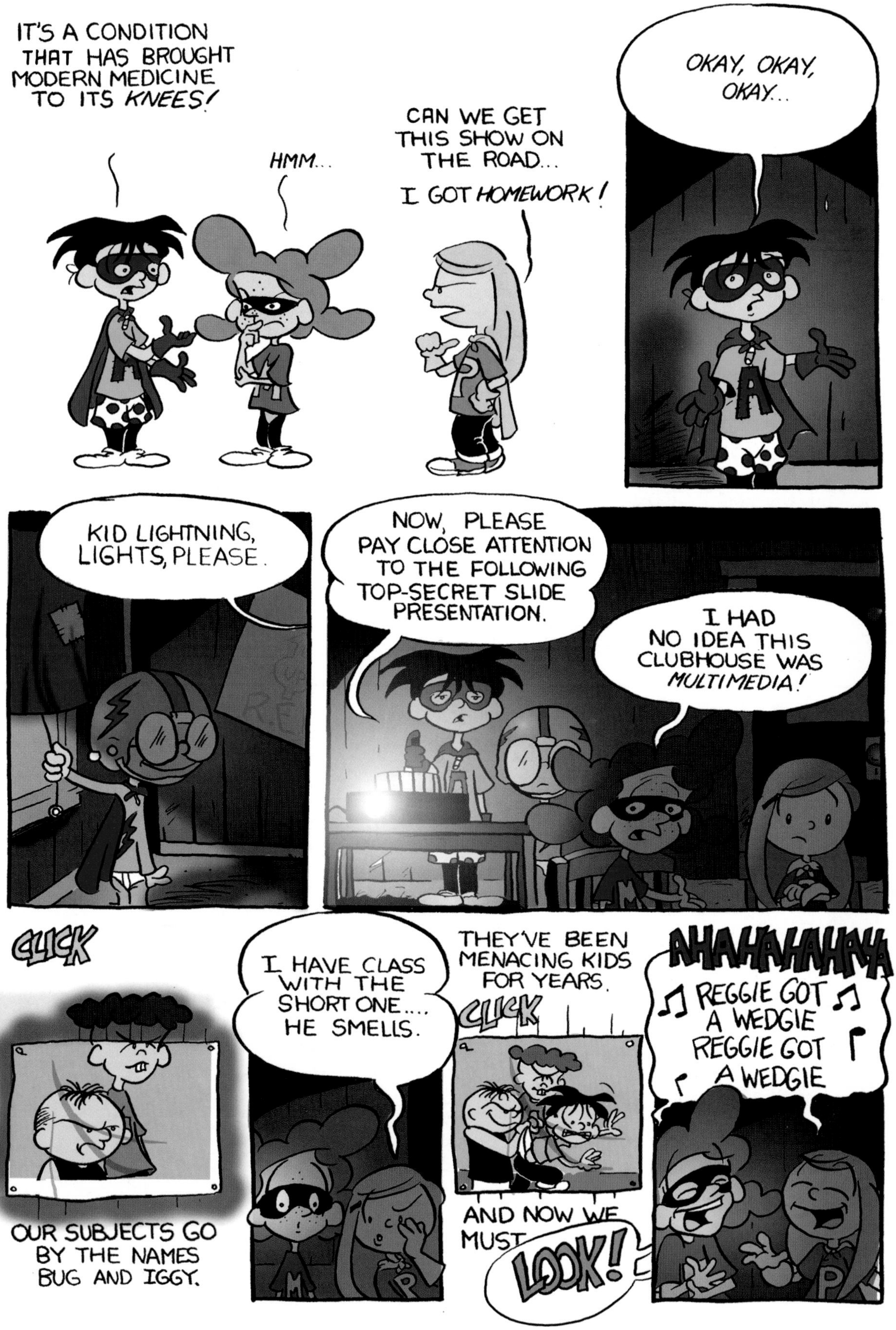
IT'S A CONDITION THAT HAS BROUGHT MODERN MEDICINE TO ITS *KNEES!*
HMM...
CAN WE GET THIS SHOW ON THE ROAD...
I GOT *HOMEWORK!*
OKAY, OKAY, OKAY...
KID LIGHTNING, LIGHTS, PLEASE.
NOW, PLEASE PAY CLOSE ATTENTION TO THE FOLLOWING TOP-SECRET SLIDE PRESENTATION.
I HAD NO IDEA THIS CLUBHOUSE WAS *MULTIMEDIA!*
CLICK
OUR SUBJECTS GO BY THE NAMES BUG AND IGGY.
I HAVE CLASS WITH THE SHORT ONE.... HE SMELLS.
THEY'VE BEEN MENACING KIDS FOR YEARS.
CLICK
AND NOW WE MUST
LOOK!
AHAHAHAHAHAHA
REGGIE GOT A WEDGIE
REGGIE GOT A WEDGIE

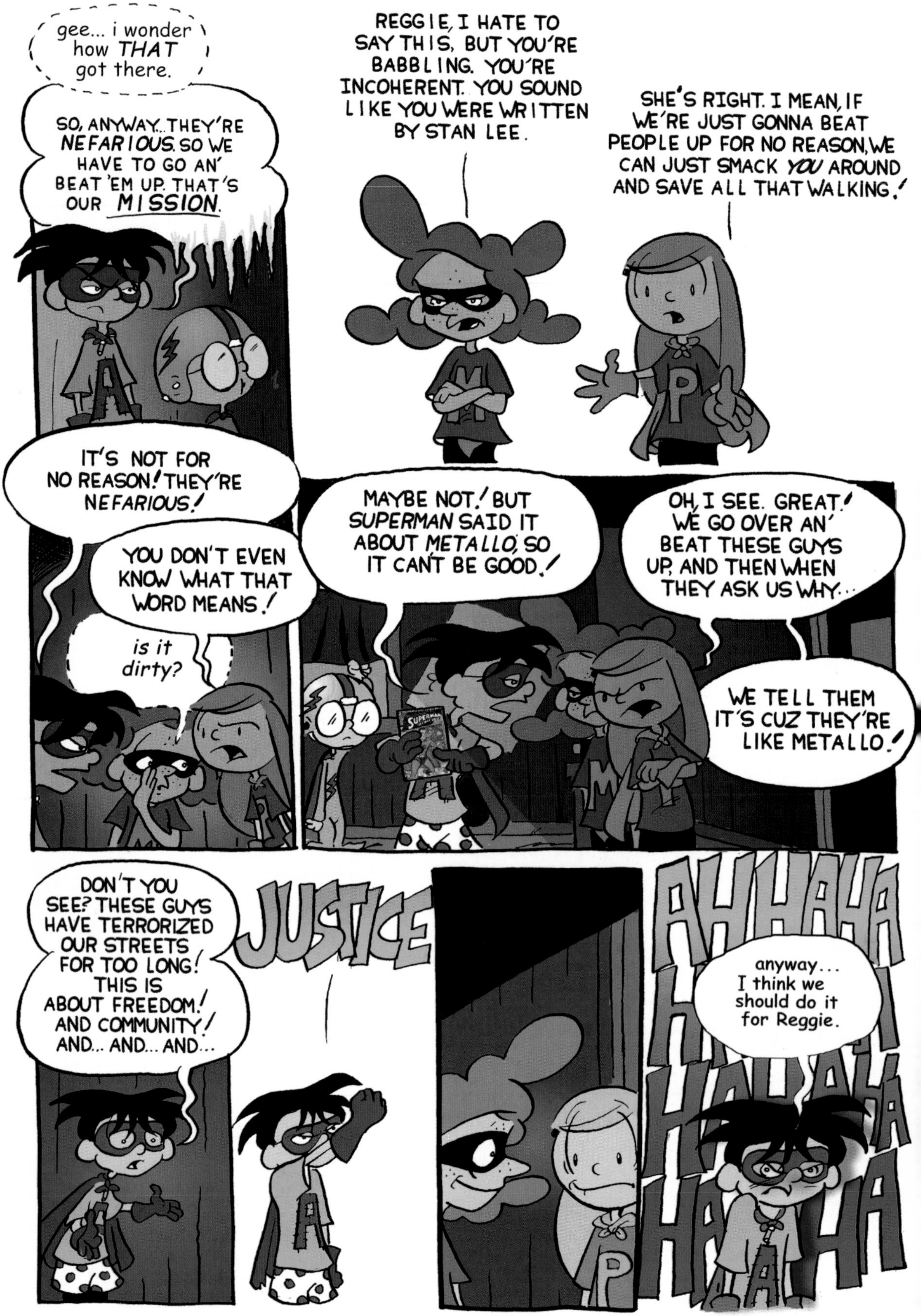
gee... i wonder how THAT got there.
SO, ANYWAY...THEY'RE NEFARIOUS. SO WE HAVE TO GO AN' BEAT 'EM UP. THAT'S OUR MISSION.
REGGIE, I HATE TO SAY THIS, BUT YOU'RE BABBLING. YOU'RE INCOHERENT. YOU SOUND LIKE YOU WERE WRITTEN BY STAN LEE.
SHE'S RIGHT. I MEAN, IF WE'RE JUST GONNA BEAT PEOPLE UP FOR NO REASON, WE CAN JUST SMACK YOU AROUND AND SAVE ALL THAT WALKING!
IT'S NOT FOR NO REASON! THEY'RE NEFARIOUS!
YOU DON'T EVEN KNOW WHAT THAT WORD MEANS!
is it dirty?
MAYBE NOT! BUT SUPERMAN SAID IT ABOUT METALLO, SO IT CAN'T BE GOOD!
OH, I SEE. GREAT! WE GO OVER AN' BEAT THESE GUYS UP, AND THEN WHEN THEY ASK US WHY...
WE TELL THEM IT'S CUZ THEY'RE LIKE METALLO!
DON'T YOU SEE? THESE GUYS HAVE TERRORIZED OUR STREETS FOR TOO LONG! THIS IS ABOUT FREEDOM! AND COMMUNITY! AND... AND... AND...
JUSTICE
AHHAHA
HAHA
HAHAHA
anyway... I think we should do it for Reggie.

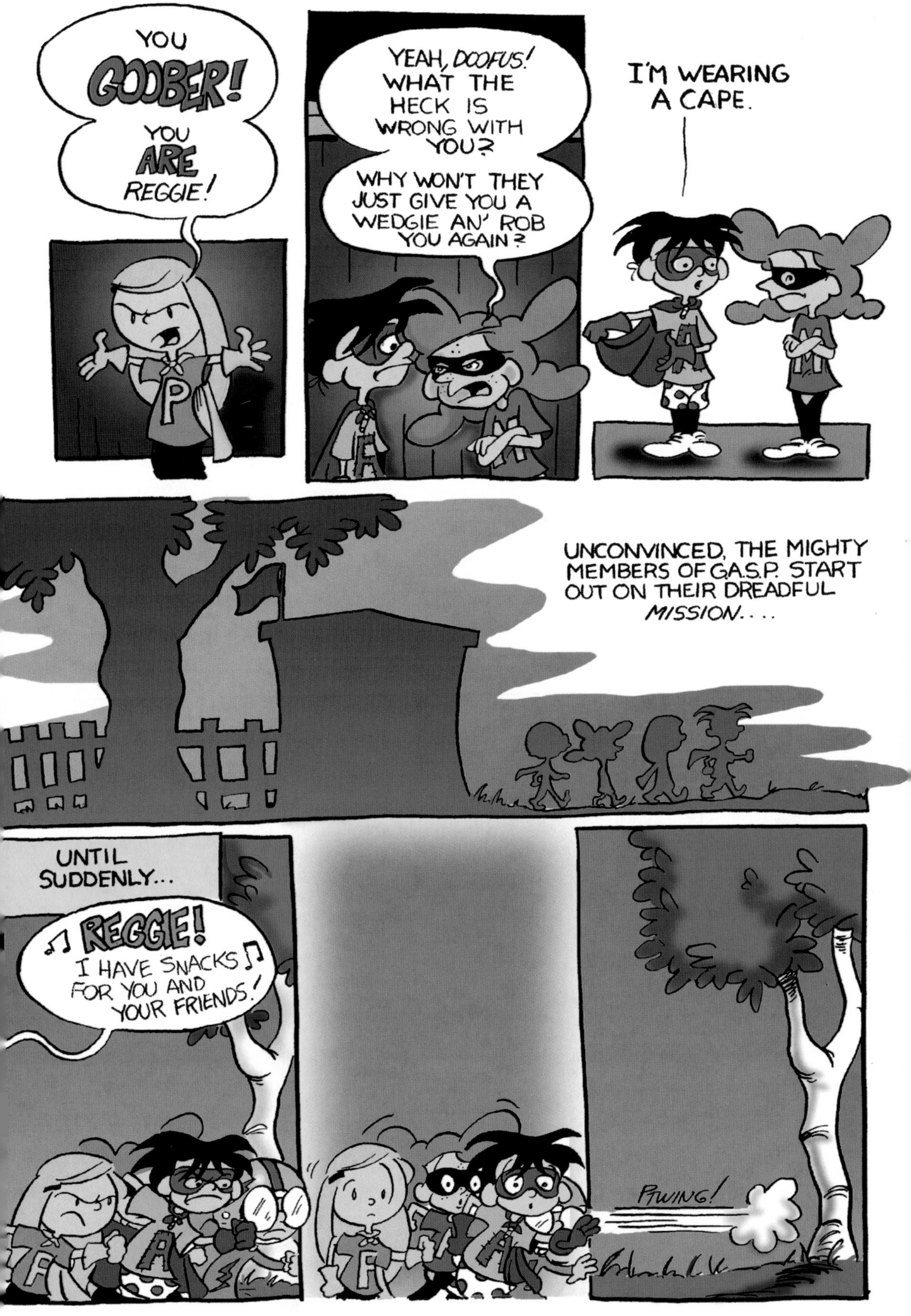
YOU GOOBER! YOU ARE REGGIE!
YEAH, DOOFUS! WHAT THE HECK IS WRONG WITH YOU?
WHY WON'T THEY JUST GIVE YOU A WEDGIE AN' ROB YOU AGAIN?
I'M WEARING A CAPE.
UNCONVINCED, THE MIGHTY MEMBERS OF G.A.S.P. START OUT ON THEIR DREADFUL MISSION....
UNTIL SUDDENLY...
REGGIE! I HAVE SNACKS FOR YOU AND YOUR FRIENDS!
PTWING!

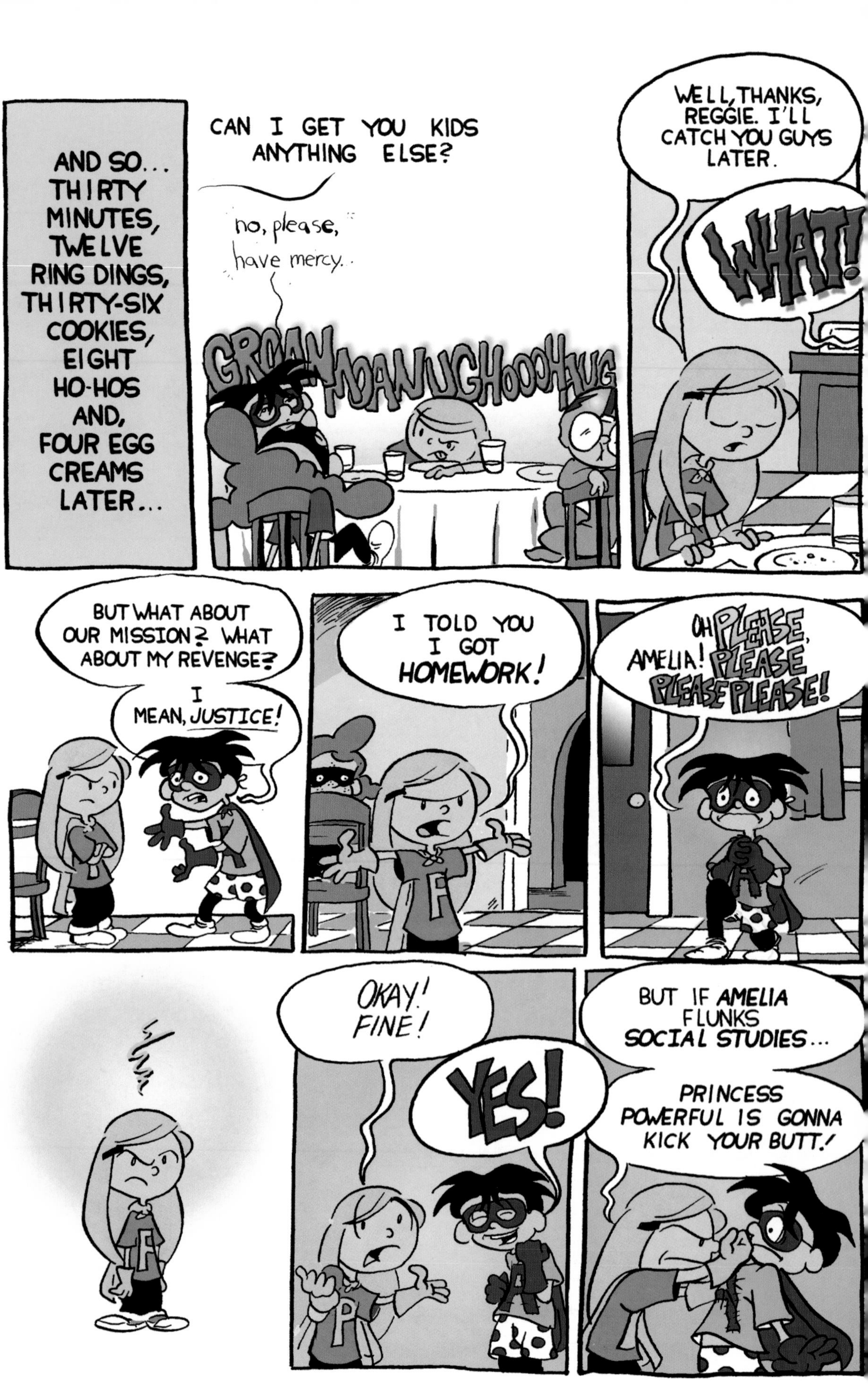
AND SO... THIRTY MINUTES, TWELVE RING DINGS, THIRTY-SIX COOKIES, EIGHT HO-HOS AND, FOUR EGG CREAMS LATER...
CAN I GET YOU KIDS ANYTHING ELSE?
no, please, have mercy...
GROAN MOAN UGH OOOH AUG
WELL, THANKS, REGGIE. I'LL CATCH YOU GUYS LATER.
WHAT!
BUT WHAT ABOUT OUR MISSION? WHAT ABOUT MY REVENGE?
I MEAN, JUSTICE!
I TOLD YOU I GOT HOMEWORK!
OH PLEASE, AMELIA! PLEASE PLEASE PLEASE!
OKAY! FINE!
YES!
BUT IF AMELIA FLUNKS SOCIAL STUDIES...
PRINCESS POWERFUL IS GONNA KICK YOUR BUTT!

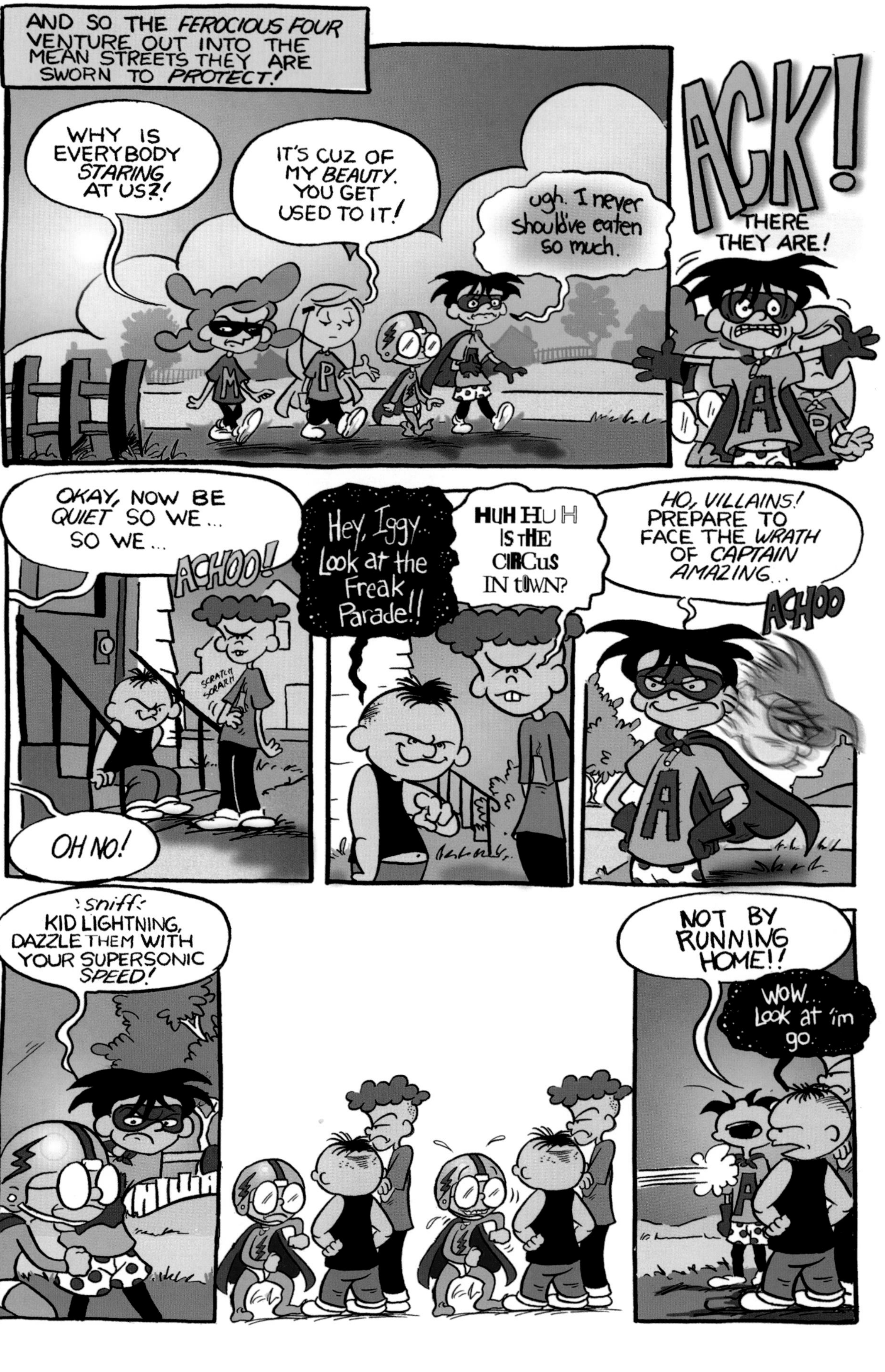
AND SO THE FEROCIOUS FOUR VENTURE OUT INTO THE MEAN STREETS THEY ARE SWORN TO PROTECT!
WHY IS EVERYBODY STARING AT US?!
IT'S CUZ OF MY BEAUTY. YOU GET USED TO IT!
ugh. I never should've eaten so much.
ACK!
THERE THEY ARE!
OKAY, NOW BE QUIET SO WE... SO WE...
ACHOO!
SCRATCH SCRATCH
OH NO!
Hey, Iggy. Look at the Freak Parade!!
HUH HUH IS THE CIRCUS IN TOWN?
HO, VILLAINS! PREPARE TO FACE THE WRATH OF CAPTAIN AMAZING...
ACHOO
:sniff:
KID LIGHTNING, DAZZLE THEM WITH YOUR SUPERSONIC SPEED!
NOT BY RUNNING HOME!!
WOW. Look at 'im go.

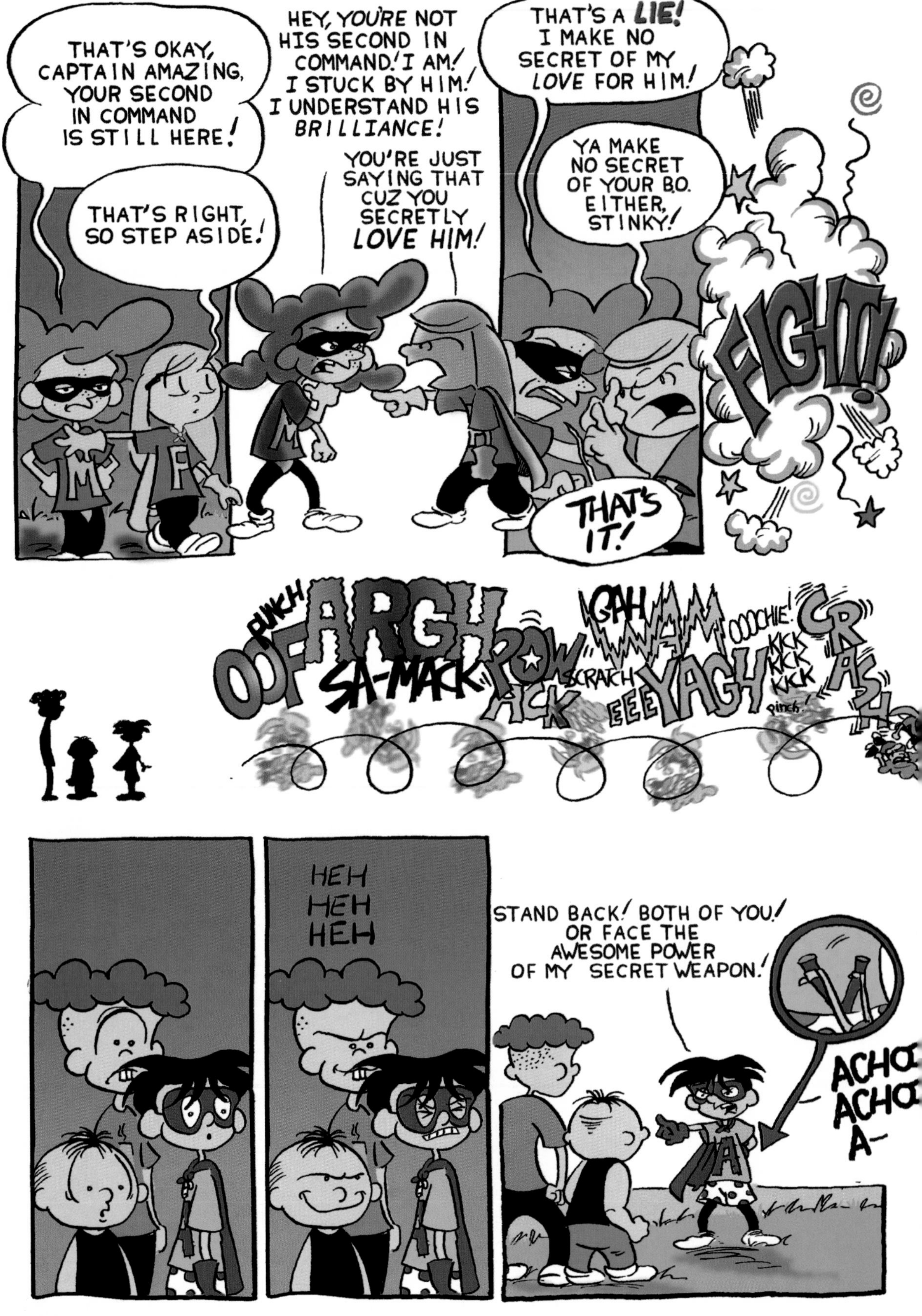
THAT'S OKAY, CAPTAIN AMAZING, YOUR SECOND IN COMMAND IS STILL HERE!
THAT'S RIGHT, SO STEP ASIDE!
HEY, YOU'RE NOT HIS SECOND IN COMMAND! I AM! I STUCK BY HIM! I UNDERSTAND HIS BRILLIANCE!
YOU'RE JUST SAYING THAT CUZ YOU SECRETLY LOVE HIM!
THAT'S A LIE! I MAKE NO SECRET OF MY LOVE FOR HIM!
YA MAKE NO SECRET OF YOUR B.O. EITHER, STINKY!
THAT'S IT!
FIGHT!
PUNCH
OOF
ARGH
SA-MACK
POW
ACK
GAH
WAM
SCRATCH
EEE
YAGH
OOOCHIE!
KKCK KKCK KKCK
pinch!
CR
ASH
HEH HEH HEH
STAND BACK! BOTH OF YOU! OR FACE THE AWESOME POWER OF MY SECRET WEAPON!
ACHOO ACHOO A-

NO ONE'S CERTAIN WHAT HAPPENED NEXT. PERHAPS IT WAS THE GLARING LATE AFTERNOON SUN. PERHAPS IT WAS THE ALLERGIES. IT ALMOST CERTAINLY WAS THE SNACK FOOD. REGARDLESS, THE NEXT INSTANT WOULD BE BURNED INTO THESE FIVE YOUNG MINDS ... FOREVER.

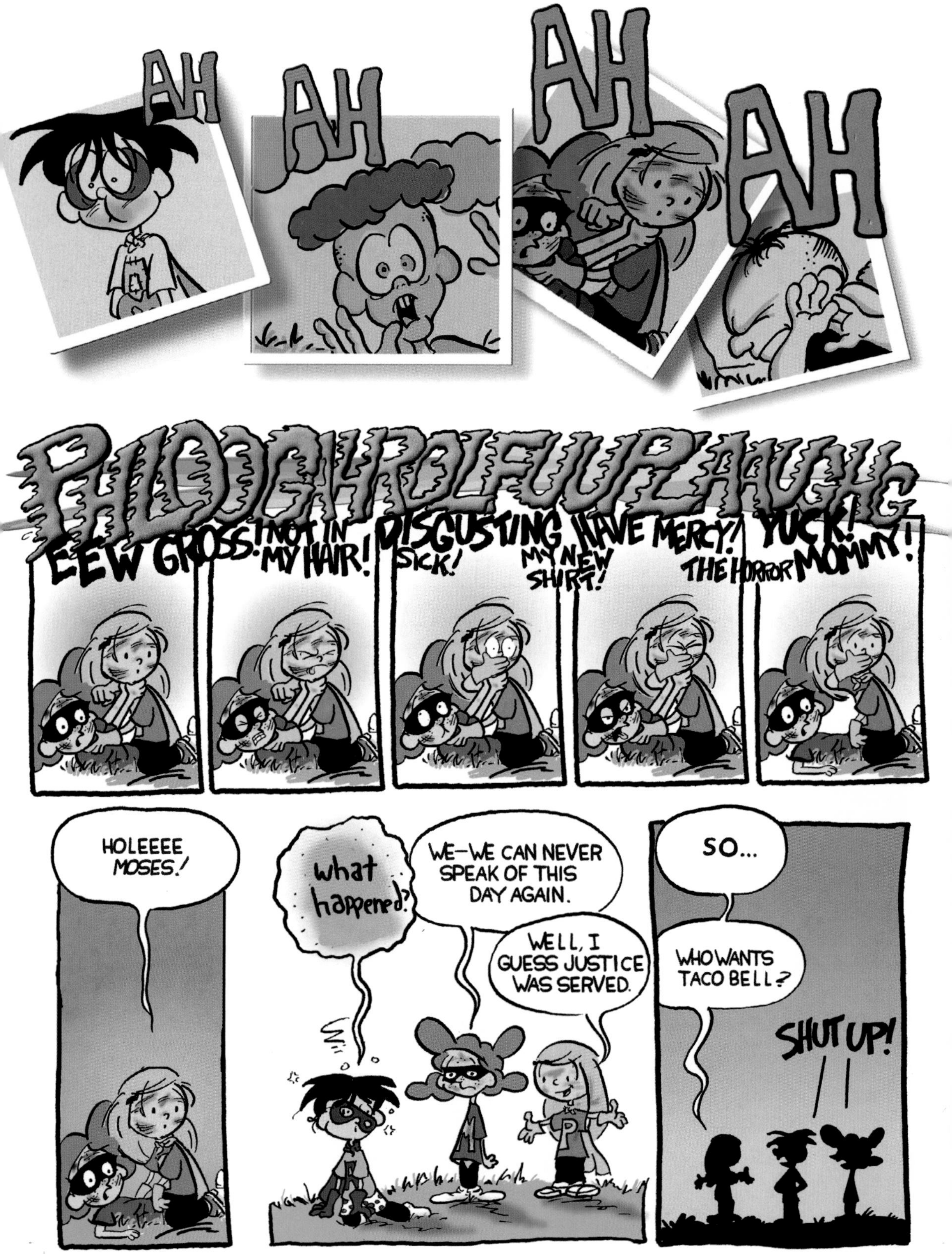
AH
AH
AH
AH
PHLOOGHROLFUUPZAUGHG
EEW GROSS!
NOT IN MY HAIR!
DISGUSTING
SICK!
HAVE MERCY!
MY NEW SHIRT!
YUCK!
THE HORROR
MOMMY!
HOLEEEE MOSES!
what happened?
WE—WE CAN NEVER SPEAK OF THIS DAY AGAIN.
WELL, I GUESS JUSTICE WAS SERVED.
SO...
WHO WANTS TACO BELL?
SHUT UP!

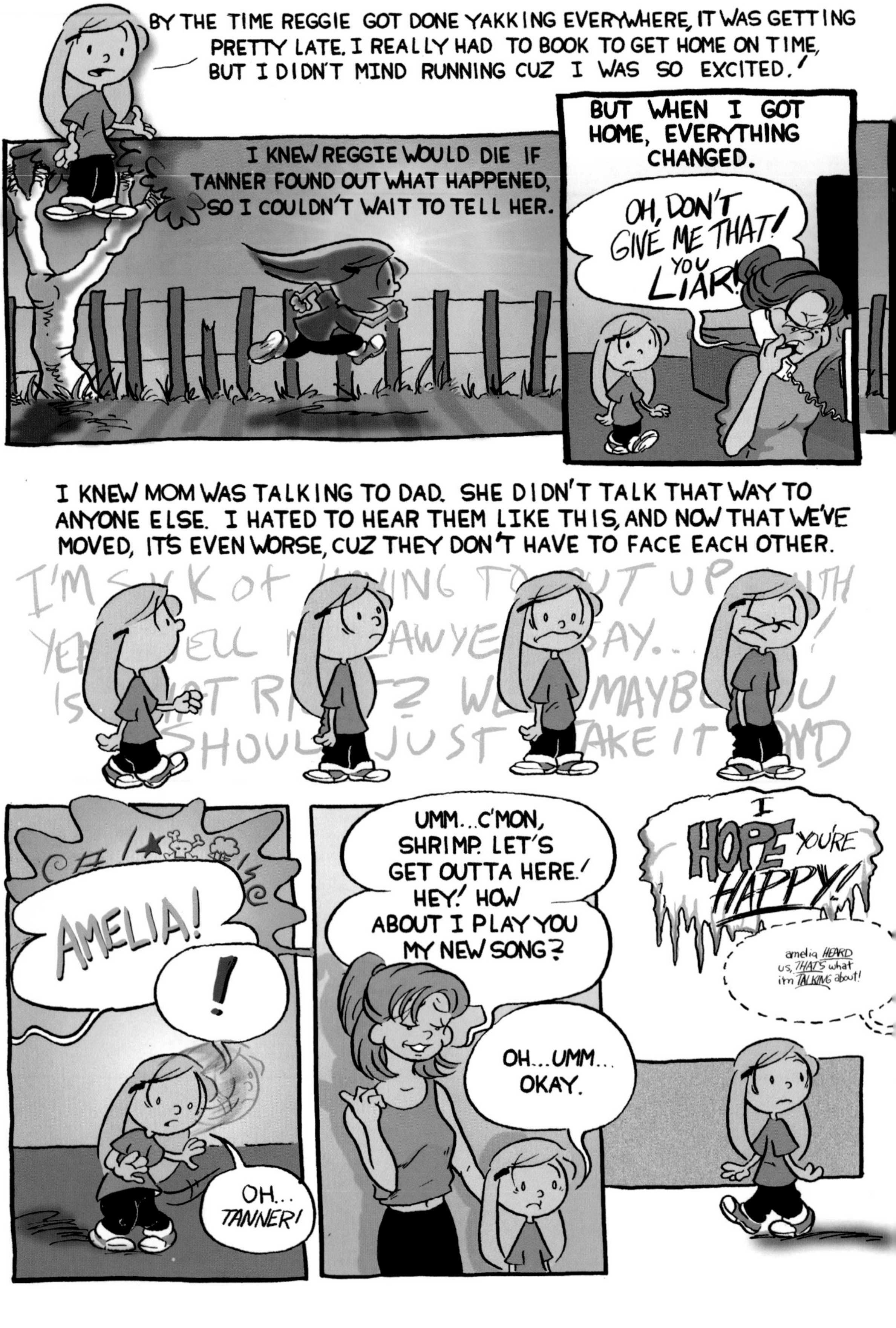
BY THE TIME REGGIE GOT DONE YAKKING EVERYWHERE, IT WAS GETTING PRETTY LATE. I REALLY HAD TO BOOK TO GET HOME ON TIME, BUT I DIDN'T MIND RUNNING CUZ I WAS SO EXCITED!
I KNEW REGGIE WOULD DIE IF TANNER FOUND OUT WHAT HAPPENED, SO I COULDN'T WAIT TO TELL HER.
BUT WHEN I GOT HOME, EVERYTHING CHANGED.
OH, DON'T GIVE ME THAT! YOU LIAR!
I KNEW MOM WAS TALKING TO DAD. SHE DIDN'T TALK THAT WAY TO ANYONE ELSE. I HATED TO HEAR THEM LIKE THIS, AND NOW THAT WE'VE MOVED, IT'S EVEN WORSE, CUZ THEY DON'T HAVE TO FACE EACH OTHER.
AMELIA!
!
OH... TANNER!
UMM...C'MON, SHRIMP. LET'S GET OUTTA HERE! HEY! HOW ABOUT I PLAY YOU MY NEW SONG?
OH...UMM... OKAY.
I HOPE YOU'RE HAPPY!
amelia HEARD us, THAT'S what i'm TALKING about!

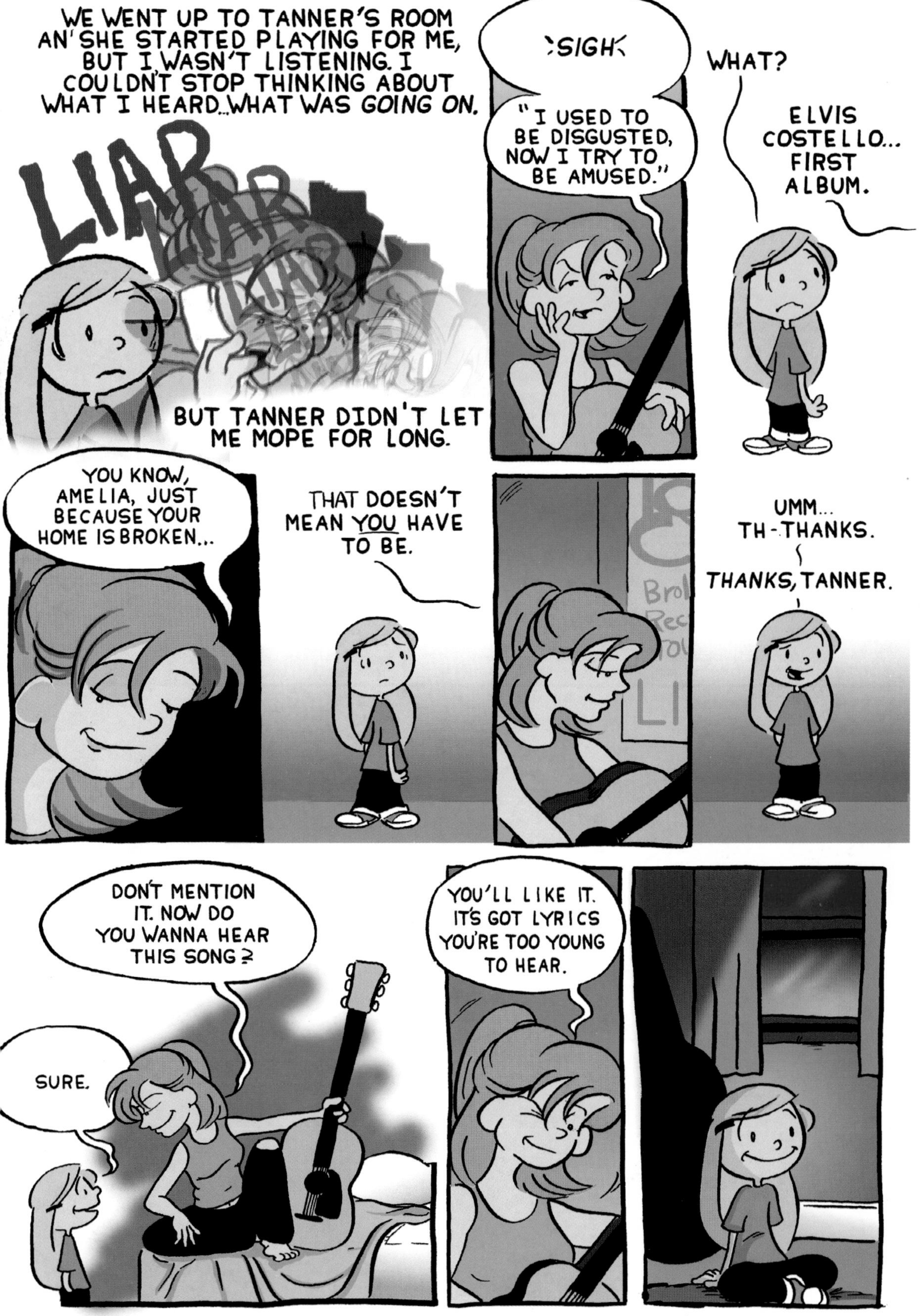

WE WENT UP TO TANNER'S ROOM AN' SHE STARTED PLAYING FOR ME, BUT I WASN'T LISTENING. I COULDN'T STOP THINKING ABOUT WHAT I HEARD...WHAT WAS GOING ON.
LIAR
BUT TANNER DIDN'T LET ME MOPE FOR LONG.
SIGH
"I USED TO BE DISGUSTED, NOW I TRY TO BE AMUSED."
WHAT?
ELVIS COSTELLO... FIRST ALBUM.
YOU KNOW, AMELIA, JUST BECAUSE YOUR HOME IS BROKEN...
THAT DOESN'T MEAN YOU HAVE TO BE.
UMM... TH-THANKS.
THANKS, TANNER.
DON'T MENTION IT. NOW DO YOU WANNA HEAR THIS SONG?
SURE.
YOU'LL LIKE IT. IT'S GOT LYRICS YOU'RE TOO YOUNG TO HEAR.

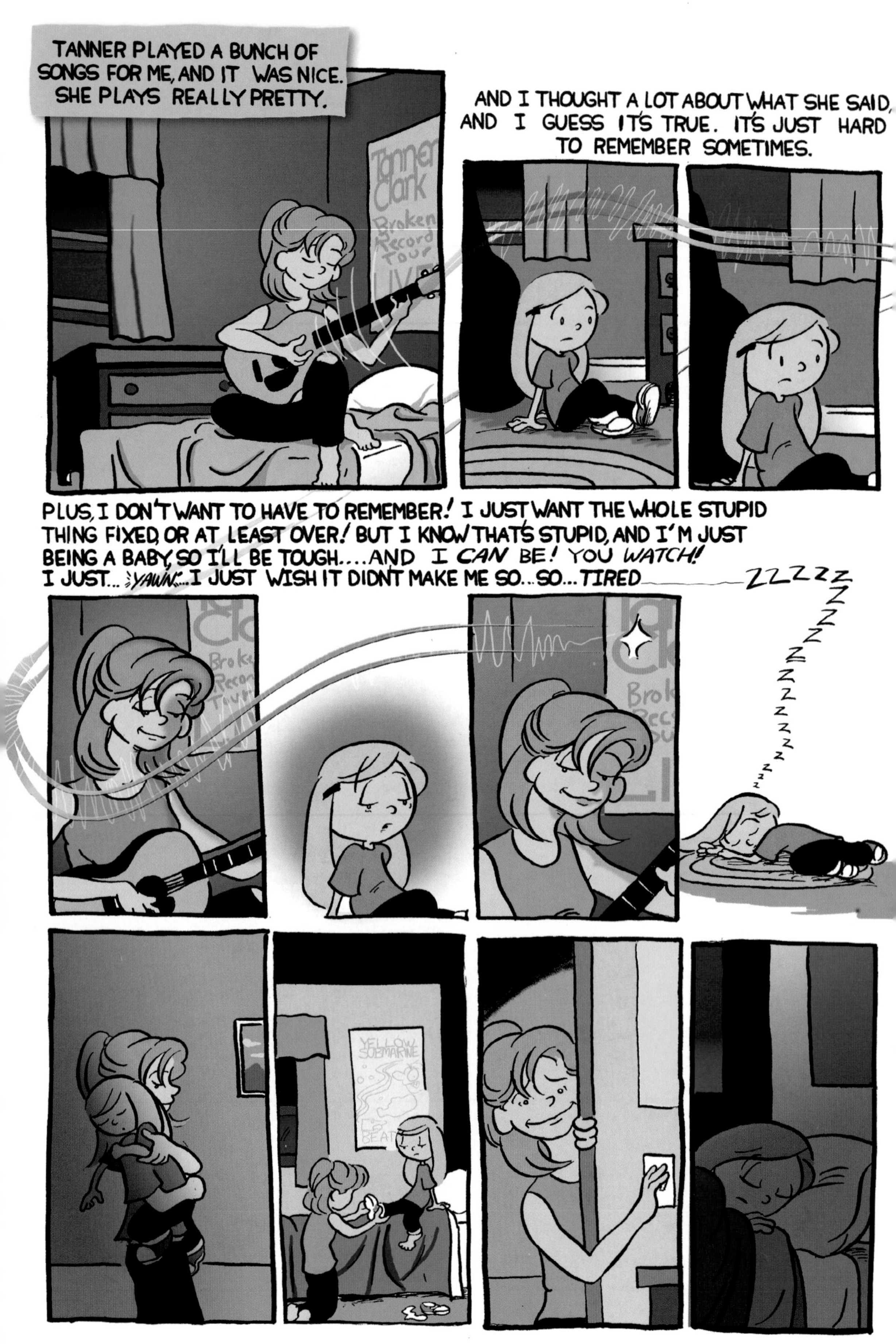
TANNER PLAYED A BUNCH OF SONGS FOR ME, AND IT WAS NICE. SHE PLAYS REALLY PRETTY.
Tanner Clark Broken Record Tour LIVE
AND I THOUGHT A LOT ABOUT WHAT SHE SAID, AND I GUESS IT'S TRUE. IT'S JUST HARD TO REMEMBER SOMETIMES.
PLUS, I DON'T WANT TO HAVE TO REMEMBER! I JUST WANT THE WHOLE STUPID THING FIXED, OR AT LEAST OVER! BUT I KNOW THAT'S STUPID, AND I'M JUST BEING A BABY, SO I'LL BE TOUGH....AND I CAN BE! YOU WATCH!
I JUST... YAWN...I JUST WISH IT DIDN'T MAKE ME SO...SO...TIRED
ZZZZZ
YELLOW SUBMARINE
BEATLES

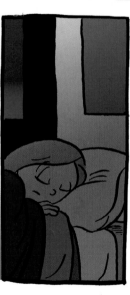